Can a boy and a dragon be friends?

THE DRAGONLING COLLECTOR'S EDITION, VOL. I

The Dragonling

To save the helpless dragonling Zantor, Darek must venture into the fearsome Valley of Dragons, risking his life to return his friend to his own fire-breathing kind!

A Dragon in the Family

It's not easy protecting a dragon! All of the villagers have turned against Darek and his family. How can he prove that dragons are good neighbors?

Dragon Quest

Zantor the dragonling is everyone's darling, and the Chief Elder's spoiled daughter wants one of her own—even though that means a dragon mother will have to die. How can Darek stop the villagers . . . unless he *joins* the dragon quest?

The Dragonling series
by Jackie French Koller

THE DRAGONLING COLLECTOR'S EDITION, Vol. 1

THE DRAGONLING COLLECTOR'S EDITION, Vol. 2

The Dragonling

COLLECTOR'S EDITION

VOL. 1

THE DRAGONLING ✦ A DRAGON IN THE FAMILY ✦ DRAGON QUEST

JACKIE FRENCH KOLLER

Aladdin Paperbacks
New York   London   Toronto   Sydney   Singapore

Dragonling text copyright © 1990 by Jackie French Koller
Dragonling illustrations copyright © 1990 by Judith Mitchell
Dragon in the Family text copyright © 1993 by Jackie French Koller
Dragon in the Family illustrations copyright © 1993 by Judith Mitchell
Dragon Quest text copyright © 1997 by Jackie French Koller
Dragon Quest illustrations copyright © 1997 by Judith Mitchell

These titles were previously published individually.

First Aladdin Paperbacks edition February 2003
First Minstrel Paperbacks edition October 2000

ALADDIN PAPERBACKS
An imprint of Simon & Schuster
Children's Publishing Division
1230 Avenue of the Americas
New York, NY 10020

Printed in the United States of America

10 9 8 7 6 5

ISBN 0-7434-1019-X

The Dragonling

To Devin,
because dragons are his second favorite animals,
next to dogs

1

Darek awoke at the first light of dawn. He sat up quickly and pushed his bed curtains aside. Through his window he could see the soft, violet rays of the morning sun just touching the tips of the yellow mountains of Orr. His brother, Clep, was up there somewhere, probably breaking camp, getting ready for the day's hunt. It wasn't fair, Darek thought. Why did he have to wait three more years before *his* first dragonquest? So what if Clep was twelve and he was only nine. He was nearly as tall and strong as Clep. Three more years! It seemed like forever.

"Darek? Darek, are you up?" It was his mother's voice from the kitchen below.

"I'm coming," Darek called back. He got dressed and clattered down the stairs.

His mother was bent over the hearth, spooning porridge into his bowl. Darek slid into his place at the table.

"Do you think maybe the men will be home today?" he asked.

His mother's brow wrinkled with worry as she served him his breakfast.

"Who knows how long they will be gone?" she said. "Ten days? Twenty? A dragonquest ends when it ends."

"I can't wait until it's my turn," Darek said eagerly. "I will be the one to make the kill. I will win the claws to wear around my neck. I will be the Marksman, like Father."

Darek's mother shook her head and turned back to the fire.

"Why are you silent, Mother?" Darek asked. "Why don't you get excited about the dragonquest like everyone else?"

"My brother was killed on his dragonquest," said Darek's mother quietly.

"Many have been killed on the dragonquests," said Darek, "but they are heroes. You should be proud."

Darek's mother sighed. "In the old days," she said, "when the dragons were plentiful, when they threatened the villages and raided the yuke* herds, that was the time for heroes. Now the dragons are few, and they keep to the mountains. Why should we send young boys into their midst?"

"They are not boys," said Darek. "They are men, and they must face a dragon to prove it."

"There are other ways to prove you are a man," said Darek's mother.

*yuke: a white, long-haired animal, much like a goat, only larger.

"What are they then?" asked Darek.

"Doing your work with pride, caring for others, and thinking your own thoughts are good ways," said Darek's mother.

"*Bah,*" said Darek. "Anyone can do those things, but only a man can slay a dragon."

There was a sudden, loud clanging and Darek's mother's head jerked up.

"The men return," she said.

Darek and his mother ran to the village square. The hunting party was threading its way down through the mountain pass, pulling a great wagon. Upon it lay a hulking mound.

"A Blue!" shouted Darek. "It's a Great Blue!" Great Blues were the largest and fiercest of all dragons. Darek could hardly contain his excitement as he raced to meet the party. But as he drew closer, his steps faltered. He could see that his father was leading a yuke, and slung over the yuke's saddle was a small

body, about the size of Clep's. Darek heard his mother cry out behind him.

Other children jostled Darek as they rushed by. "What's the matter? Hurry up! Get out of the way!" Darek swallowed hard and tried to ignore the great weight that had settled in his chest. If it *was* Clep he must be brave. He must not shed a tear. He must be honored to have a hero for a brother.

Then a voice called out. "Darek! Mother! Over here!" A yuke broke out of the hunting party, and Darek saw that its rider was Clep. Relief rushed over him as he ran to meet his brother.

Clep swung himself down out of the saddle. He held up a necklace. A necklace made of claws! "I made the kill!" he shouted. "I killed a Great Blue!"

Darek fought back a pang of jealousy. "I can't believe it!" he shouted, thumping Clep on the back. "You? The Marksman!"

Darek's mother came up beside them.

There was joy and relief in her eyes as she hugged Clep tightly to her, but when he held up the bloodstained necklace, she looked away.

"Who is the fallen one?" she asked quietly.

Clep's face grew grave. "It is Yoran," he said.

The weight came back to Darek's chest. Yoran? Clep's best friend? Yoran, who had been like a second brother in their house ever since Darek could remember? Yoran, who ran faster than the wind? How could it be he who lay so still now across the saddle?

Darek's mother nodded, her face like stone. "I must go to his mother," she said.

2

Darek couldn't sleep. He was too excited about the festival tomorrow. His brother, Clep, and all of their family would be the guests of honor. There would be dancing and feasting, and then at night, a great bonfire in which the body of the dragon would be burned. Now it lay on the wagon, just outside the paddock fence. Tomorrow night its ashes would be placed in a carved urn and given to Clep. Clep would place the urn on the mantel, next to his father's. One day Darek vowed to place an urn there too.

Outside, in the paddock, Darek could hear the nervous rustling of the yukes. It made them uneasy to have the body of the dragon so near. Darek listened. The house was still. No one would know if he went down to comfort Nonni, his favorite, and gave her a bit of sugar. He crept out in his nightshirt.

"Here, Nonni, little pet," he whispered. The small yuke ran to his side and nuzzled him gently. Darek took the sugar from his pocket and fed it to her. Her rough, wet tongue tickled his hand as she licked every crumb from between his fingers.

Darek stared at the great dragon. He could see it clearly in the light of Zoriak's twin moons. It lay on its side, its wings twisted and crumpled, its once fearsome claws stubby and blunt. Darek got goose bumps thinking about how it must have looked in life. He walked around it, imagining it standing on its powerful legs, flames shooting from its mouth. He could see it charge. He could hear it roar. He could hear it . . . whimper?

Darek jumped back. He was sure he had heard something. Could the creature still be alive? Darek wasn't taking any chances. He dived for cover behind a barliberry bush and lay still, waiting. The sound came again, *huf-uh huf-uh,* a soft hiccuping kind of sob. Darek peeked out. The great head lay just in front of him, still as death. He crept out of hiding and circled the creature once again. Then he saw it — a tiny head peeking out of the pouch on the giant dragon's belly. *A dragonling!*

Darek stared in amazement. He knew dragons carried their young in pouches until they were old enough to fend for themselves, but he had never seen a live dragonling before. The small creature came out of the pouch and climbed unsteadily up its mother's chest. It was about half as big as Darek, and he guessed it to be very young, maybe even new-born.

The dragonling licked its mother's still face with its forked tongue, whimpering all the while. Darek stepped back and slipped on a pebble, falling to the ground. The dragonling twisted its neck and looked at him, its eyes shining pale green in the night.

"*Rrronk,*" it said and began to climb down in his direction.

Darek scrambled to his feet. Small as the creature was, it was still a dragon, and Darek had no wish to face it unarmed. He picked up a big stick. The dragonling fluttered down off the wagon and approached on wobbly legs.

"*Rrronk,*" it said again.

Darek held the stick out like a sword. The dragonling stopped and sniffed it. It gave it a lick, then whimpered again. Darek had been taught all his life to hate and fear dragons, but it was hard to hate such a small one, and

an orphan at that. He lowered his club, and the dragonling came up and nuzzled him.

Darek felt in his pocket. There was a small lump of sugar left. He held it out cautiously. The little dragon sniffed it, then the forked tongue flicked out, and it was gone.

"*Thrrummmm,*" said the dragon. It was a happy sound. The dragon nuzzled him again.

"I don't have any more," said Darek, holding both hands up. "See?"

The dragon butted him playfully.

"All right, all right," said Darek. "I'll get more. Wait here." He turned and started toward the house. The dragon wobbled after him.

"No," said Darek, quickening his steps. "You stay."

"*Rrronk,*" said the dragon. It flapped its small wings and flew a few feet to catch up.

Darek stopped and stared at it, suddenly realizing what he'd done. He'd made friends with a dragon, an enemy of his people. Now what was he supposed to do?

3

Darek struggled to close the barn door, pushing the dragonling back in.

"You've got to wait here," he said. "And don't make a sound."

"*Rrronk*," said the dragon.

"You don't understand," said Darek. "They'll kill you if they find you." He gave a final push, then pulled the door tight and lowered the latch. He could hear the orphan's muffled whimpers on the other side. He had to hurry or someone else might wake and hear.

Darek crept up to his room, dressed quickly, then tiptoed down to the back room where the weapons were kept. He slung his bow over his shoulder and strapped his quiver of arrows in place. On his way through the kitchen he filled a sack with supplies. It would be a journey of many days.

Suddenly he stopped and wondered. What do dragonlings eat? Perhaps such a young one would still need milk. He would have to bring along a female yuke. Dorlass, whose calf had been born dead, had milk to spare, but she would not nurse a dragonling. Darek packed a waterskin so he could feed the creature by hand.

Darek paused in the kitchen doorway and looked back. His stomach twisted into a knot. What was he doing, anyway? What would his father say? Risking his life to save a dragon? An enemy of his people? A dragon that *he* might even have to face one day on his own dragonquest? He could still turn back. It was not too late. Perhaps he should just let the creature be found and killed. After all, what more did a dragon deserve?

Darek walked slowly out to the barn. The soft, hiccuping sound still came from inside. He opened the door and the dragonling rushed out and rubbed happily against him.

"*Thrrummm, thrrummmm, thrrummmm,*" it said.

Darek stroked its scaly head. "Why did you have to come here?" he whispered. Then he looked over at the lifeless body of the Great Blue. "I guess it wasn't your idea either, was it? Come then. I'll take you home, but after that I never want to see you again, understand?"

The dragonling thrummed happily. Darek took out another lump of sugar and let the orphan lick it from his hand. The sky was slowly growing lighter.

"Come on," said Darek, "we've got to go."

He led Dorlass out of the paddock. She was

skittish around the dragonling. It kept running in and out between her legs, making her buck and jump while Darek was trying to get her saddle pack strapped on.

"Cut that out," said Darek, giving the dragonling a gentle kick.

"*Rrronk, rrronk, rrronk,*" it screeched, then it half ran, half flew back up to its mother's body and dove into her pouch.

Darek finished securing the saddle, then he led Dorlass over to the Great Blue. "Hey," he whispered, "come on out of there."

He saw a lump wiggle around in the pouch, but the dragonling did not appear.

"Come on, don't be such a baby," Darek coaxed. "I hardly even touched you."

The dragonling poked its head out. "*Rrronk,*" it said.

"I'm sorry," said Darek. "I thought dragons were tough."

He held out another piece of sugar, and the dragon crept slowly down again. Darek fed it and scratched its head until it was thrumming happily. "Some fighter you're going to make," he whispered.

Darek led Dorlass out to the road. The dragonling followed.

"You're going to have to move faster than that," said Darek, "if we're going to get to the pass before sunrise." He ran forward a few steps and then called to the dragonling. It flapped its wings and flew to catch up. Running and calling, running and calling, Darek managed to get to the foothills just as the first rays of the sun peeked over the mountaintops. Suddenly the little dragon turned back.

"Where are you going?" yelled Darek. He ran after the dragonling and grabbed it gently by the wings. It struggled to get away.

"*Rrronk,*" it squawked, "*rrronk!*"

It was staring back down the hill at the body of its mother.

Darek stroked its head.

"I know," he said. "It is *rrronk.*"

4

"I guess if we're going to be together awhile I ought to give you a name," said Darek. "Are you a boy or a girl?"

The little creature didn't answer. It had spied an insect of some kind on the path, and it was all bent over, nose to the ground. Suddenly the insect bit it.

"*Rrronk, rrronk,*" it screeched, running over and shoving its head up under Darek's shirt.

"Will you get out of here!" yelled Darek, giving the creature a push and pulling his shirt back down. "I'm not your mother and I don't have a pouch."

The dragonling lay down and curled itself around his legs.

"You're the sorriest excuse for a dragon I've ever seen," Darek said, peeling the orphan off his legs. Then he noticed its belly.

"You don't have a pouch either," he said. "That means you must be a boy."

"*Huf-uh, huf-uh*," the dragonling sobbed, rubbing its nose with its forefoot.

"It's only a bug bite, for pity's sake," said Darek. "You have to toughen up. I'll give you a strong name, a powerful name. Then maybe you'll try a little harder to live up to it. I will call you Zantor, King of the Dragons."

Zantor whimpered and pushed his head under Darek's arm. "Well," Darek said, "maybe you'll grow into it."

By evening Zantor was moving very slowly and stumbling often.

"It's been a long day for you, hasn't it?"

said Darek. "We'll stop now and camp for the night."

Zantor moaned softly and nuzzled Darek's pocket.

"The sugar is all gone," said Darek. "But I'll get you some milk."

He set to work milking Dorlass, and when he had filled the waterskin, he held it up over the dragonling's head. "Drink," he said, letting loose a stream.

The milk squirted in Zantor's eyes and dripped off his nose, but he made no attempt to drink it.

"Didn't your mother teach you anything?" said Darek. He opened the dragon's mouth with one hand and squirted the milk in with the other. Zantor started to sputter and choke. Darek stopped squirting, and the little dragon shook his head and spit all the milk back out.

"Look," said Darek, "it may not be your mother's, but it's all we have."

Zantor clamped his mouth shut and refused to drink.

Darek shrugged. Maybe dragons *didn't* nurse their babies. Maybe baby dragons ate regular food right away. It was worth a try. "I'll be right back," he said, shouldering his bow. "You wait here."

Darek didn't know whether Zantor understood or whether he was just too tired to move, but whatever the reason, he obeyed.

There were plenty of animals in the mountain forest, and Darek was a good shot. He quickly brought down a small glibbet* and carried it back to Zantor.

"There," he said, laying the animal at the dragon's feet. "Now eat." Darek sat down and laid out his own supper, some bread and cheese and a big cluster of barliberries.

Zantor sniffed at the glibbet, then he whimpered and began digging a hole. The next thing Darek knew, the dragonling had buried it.

*glibbet: a small, weasel-like animal

"Hey," said Darek, "what are you doing? You can't save that. You have to eat it now. We're moving on in the morning."

Darek dug the glibbet up again, but when he turned around he found Zantor happily munching on *his* barliberries.

"Well I'll be," said Darek. "You eat barliberries? What else do you eat?" He went into the woods and gathered all the herbs and nuts and berries he could find. Zantor gulped them greedily and followed him back to find more. At last they were both full, and Darek set about building a campfire. He gathered sticks and dry leaves, then he took out his flint and struck it against a rock. A spark flew out and landed on the leaves. Darek blew on it. It flared a moment, then died. Darek tried again. This time Zantor bent down, right next to him, staring intently. Darek blew on the spark. It sputtered and went out.

"Drat," said Darek. Then suddenly, *Whoosh!* A stream of flame shot by his nose.

Darek jumped back. It was Zantor! Zantor was breathing fire!

In no time at all the campfire was burning merrily. Zantor sat back on his hind legs, looking quite proud.

"Wow," said Darek. "That was pretty good. I didn't know you could do that yet."

Zantor thrummed happily, then curled up next to the campfire and went to sleep.

Darek stared at him. "You really are the strangest dragon I've ever heard of," he whispered, then he rolled his blanket out on the other side of the campfire and lay down.

The night was dark and damp, and the woods were full of strange calls and rustlings. Darek began to wish he were home in his own warm bed. He missed his family. Perhaps the little dragon felt lonely too, because before long Darek heard a soft scuffling, and then a small body nestled up against his own.

5

Darek awoke to find Zantor still snuggled up beside him.

"Sleep well?" he asked.

The dragon thrummed and licked him on the cheek.

"Will you cut that out?" said Darek. "You're supposed to be tough, remember?"

Darek made himself a breakfast of bread and barliberry jam while Zantor foraged in the woods, obviously remembering all the places Darek had shown him the night before.

"Pretty smart, aren't you?" said Darek when the dragon came back. Zantor looked healthier already. His scales, which had been dull and greenish, were now turning a shiny, peacock blue.

That day and the next two passed much like the first, except that Zantor grew stronger each day and was able to move more quickly. By the fourth day they were getting close to the Valley of the Dragons. Darek had never been there, but he had heard it described so many times around the campfire that he knew just what to look for.

"Won't be long now," he told Zantor. "You'll be home by afternoon." Zantor thrummed happily, and Darek wondered again if he somehow understood. Darek suddenly grew sad at the thought of leaving the dragonling behind. "That's what you came here for," he scolded himself angrily. "He's only a dragon, after all." But still, Darek worried. What would the other dragons think of

Zantor, with his strange and gentle ways? Would they accept him, or treat him as an outcast? Or worse, would they kill him?

Darek and Zantor came upon the twin stones that marked the entrance to the valley, and Darek realized that they must proceed carefully. He tied Dorlass to a tree, then crept up to the top of a ridge to look out over the valley. Zantor scrambled up beside him.

"Get down, stupid," said Darek, throwing an arm around Zantor's neck and pulling him down.

"*Rrronk, rrronk,*" said Zantor, struggling to get free.

"*Shhhush!*" said Darek. Then he pointed down into the valley. "Look!"

Darek's heart pounded. For all his brave talk, he was unprepared for the size and number of creatures moving about below. Some of them lazed in the sun. Others waded in the river. Smaller ones butted heads together and tumbled like children in the dirt. There were caves cut into the mountains all around the valley, and occasionally a dragon would appear at the mouth of one and glide down on great wings to the valley floor. They were mostly Yellow Crested dragons, with a few Green Horned. Darek saw no Great Blues at all.

Zantor was staring at the scene excitedly.

"Is this your home?" Darek asked him. "Where are your kind?"

Zantor turned his head and looked toward the mountain on the right, high up at the very largest caves. There was a sudden movement in the shadows, and then a Great Blue stepped full into the sun. She stood poised for a moment on the edge, then lifted off and soared out almost over their heads.

"*Thrummmm, thrummmm, thrummmm,*" said Zantor.

"*Shhush!*" whispered Darek, clamping a hand over the dragonling's mouth. Darek stared up in awe at the Great Blue. She was the most magnificent creature he had ever seen. The sun glinted on her deep blue scales, making them sparkle like the sea. Her wings stretched out silver and shimmering against the pale blue sky. For all her great size, she was sleek in the air, and when she landed gracefully on the valley floor she stood head and shoulders above the rest, like a queen.

Darek let go of Zantor's mouth. Zantor thrummed again, happily staring down at the Great Blue. Darek smiled and nodded.

"Yes," he said. "I think she would make you a fine mother."

6

Getting the Great Blue to adopt Zantor would be tricky. Zantor was not yet strong enough to fly down into the valley himself, and Darek wasn't about to *walk* him down. The best chance, he decided, would be to get the dragonling up to the Great Blue's cave while she was away. If she came home and found him in her nest, she might be more likely to accept him as her own.

Knowing what to do, and doing it, however, were two different matters. The cave was high up on the mountainside. Climbing would be difficult, and worse, they would be in plain sight of the dragons. Darek decided that they'd make the climb at night, and then hide in the bushes near the mouth of the cave until the Great Blue went out in the morning.

Darek ate a large supper of cheese and milk and bread, and then topped it off with a generous helping of berries that he and Zantor found. When the sun went down, Zantor started scuffling around, nose to the ground. He pushed a couple of sticks together and started to blow on them.

"No, Zantor," said Darek. "No campfire tonight." He picked up the sticks and tossed them into the woods. Far back down the mountain pass, a bright flicker in the darkness caught his eye.

A campfire. Darek took a deep breath and let it out slowly. It was a search party, he was sure. His father and Clep and the others had come after him. He'd been so busy thinking ahead that he'd never thought back about the trail he was leaving. He guessed them to be about a day's journey behind him. He still had a chance to make his plan work, but there would be no second chances.

Darek sat down and looked at Zantor.

"I don't know if you understand me at all," he said, "but what I have to say is very important. You and I are going up there." He pointed to himself, then to Zantor, then to the cave. "We're going now. Tonight. Do you understand?"

Zantor stared where Darek pointed. "*Rrronk,*" he said.

"It *is* going to be *rrronk,*" said Darek, "but we can make it. Just follow me, and be *quiet.*" Darek put his hand around Zantor's mouth and held it shut to show him what quiet meant, then he moved off into the darkness. The dragonling followed.

Climbing was hard and slow. Zantor seemed better at it than Darek. He was lighter, for one thing, and his claws were good at finding niches to hold on to. Darek's hands grew sore and numb from the night chill. Several times he found himself wondering again why he was risking his life for a dragon.

Suddenly there was a piercing shriek. From a cave across the valley two dragons appeared. They roared and charged at each other. Their fiery breath lit up the night. Darek flattened himself against the rock, hoping the noise wouldn't awaken the Great Blue. Zantor whimpered. The two dragons, both Yellows, went on screeching for a while, then quieted down and went back into the same cave. Darek chuckled. "Perhaps they are husband and wife," he whispered to Zantor. "I've heard arguments like that back in the village."

Darek and Zantor edged onward. They had almost reached the cave when Darek felt himself slipping. He grabbed hold of a small bush and kicked out, madly trying to find safe footing. There was none. Darek's heart sank. His hands were so sore and tired he could hardly hang on. So this was how it was going to end? His father and Clep would find him dead at the bottom of the cliffs. What a fool he'd been.

Suddenly something tugged at the back of his neck and Darek felt himself rising. He was dragged up and up until he was on firm ground again. Zantor landed beside him, breathing heavily.

"You?" said Darek. "You lifted me up, with those little wings?" Zantor seemed too tired to answer. He just laid his head in Darek's lap. Darek stroked it gently.

"Maybe you *are* growing into your name," he whispered.

7

Darek and Zantor spent the rest of the night in the bushes outside the Great Blue's cave. At the stroke of dawn, before it was even fully light, the Great Blue appeared. The whole valley quickly came to life. With great squawks and chatterings, dragons appeared at the mouth of every cave and crisscrossed down through the air. The Great Blue lifted off.

Darek sucked in his breath. "Well," he said, "I guess this is it." He edged his way out of the bushes and into the cave, motioning to Zantor to follow. The cave was pitch-black inside, and Darek couldn't see a thing, but instantly the air was filled with a chorus of *rrronks*. Dragonlings! Zantor rushed past Darek back into the gloom, and the *rrronks* turned to excited thrummings.

Darek's eyes gradually adjusted to the darkness and at last he could make out Zantor and two other slightly larger dragonlings tumbling merrily over one another. Darek smiled. He wished he could give Zantor a farewell hug, but he knew the smartest thing to do was to leave, fast. Just as he turned to go, a huge shadow darkened the mouth of the cave.

"Grrrawk! Grrrawk!" shrieked the Great Blue as she touched down on the outer ledge. Darek's blood turned to ice. She must have heard her babies cry and come back to check on them. If only he'd waited until she was out of earshot! Her great bulk filled the

entrance. Darek whirled, looking for another passageway. There was none. These were not ordinary caves, he realized, just holes in the mountains hollowed out by the dragons' sharp claws.

"*Grrrawk! Grrrawk!*" the dragon screeched again. She glared at him, her green eyes glowing in the dark. Darek swung his bow off his shoulder and reached back for an arrow. With a trembling hand he fitted it to the string. There was only one unprotected spot, he knew, high up on the neck, just under the chin. She would lift her head just before battle. He would have one chance.

The dragon reared back. Flames shot from her mouth and lit up the cave. Darek took aim and —

Whomp! Darek took a hard blow to the back. He fell forward, the wind knocked out of him. He twisted in the dirt, gulping and sucking for air. When at last he could breathe again, he rolled over. Zantor stood behind him.

"Traitor!" Darek hissed, knowing even as he said it how foolish it sounded. Wouldn't he have done the same thing in Zantor's place? The Great Blue reared back and roared again, and Darek put his head down and waited for the end.

But instead of flames, or teeth, or claws, he felt only a small pressure. Zantor had lain down on top of him.

The Great Blue stopped roaring and started pacing back and forth, as if trying to decide how to deal with this strange turn of events. Her own dragonlings came over to her and made small mewing sounds. She picked them up and dropped them gently into her pouch. Then she came over and touched noses with Zantor. He whimpered and made little mewing noises too. She licked him tenderly and he began to thrumm. She picked him up and put him into her pouch as well.

Darek was glad, at least, that the dragon had accepted Zantor. Now it was *his* turn.

With one claw the dragon ripped off Darek's quiver and tossed it over near his bow. In a mighty burst of flame the weapons disappeared. Darek cringed. With the same claw the dragon rolled him over. She sniffed him up and down and stared a long time into his eyes, then, to Darek's amazement, she hooked her claw through his shirt, picked him up, and dropped him into her pouch with the others.

Zantor nestled up against him. *"Thrrumm, thrrumm, thrrumm,"* he said. Darek let out a sigh of relief.

"I don't know what you told her," he said, "but thanks."

Darek was glad to be alive, but not at all sure what to expect next. He poked his head up. The Great Blue had turned and shuffled back out to the edge of the rock ledge. She plucked one of her dragonlings from the pouch and set him down before her.

"Grok," she said. The dragonling wobbled

for a moment on the edge, then fluttered out into the air. The dragon lifted out the second dragonling.

"Oh, no." Darek groaned. "We *would* arrive just in time for flying lessons."

After the second dragonling was airborne, the Great Blue lifted out Zantor. Zantor stood timidly on the edge, his wings sagging. "*Rrronk?*" he said.

The mother dragon nudged him gently but firmly, and off he went. Darek closed his eyes, then opened one. Zantor flapped and fluttered for a moment, then straightened out and glided beautifully.

The next thing he knew, Darek found *himself* standing on the ledge. The drop to the valley below made his head swim and his knees feel like jelly. The Great Blue bent close and eyed him up and down. Then she turned him around and eyed him up and down again. Finally she snorted, picked him up, and put him back in her pouch.

The Great Blue lifted off and soared out over the valley. The wind whipped through Darek's hair and took his breath away. The ground raced by below him. He was flying! Suddenly Darek didn't even care if the dragons killed him in the end. The thrill of this moment made it all worthwhile.

The dragon made a surprisingly gentle landing. Zantor came running over, thrumming loudly, and jumped into the pouch with Darek. "Shush," said Darek, ducking down as far as he could. He was not sure the other dragons would accept him as readily as the Great Blue had.

All of the dragons had moved into the forest — hunting, Darek imagined. The Great Blue and her two dragonlings followed. Darek peeked out. To his amazement, the dragons were not hunting at all. They were feeding on fruits and nuts and leaves, just like Zantor.

8

Darek lay back with his head resting on Zantor's round belly. The Great Blue and the dragonlings were sleeping. All of the dragons, it seemed, returned to their caves for naps at midday. Darek was drowsy too, after his long night, but he was too excited to sleep. His mind was running in leaps and bounds. If the Zorians could befriend these dragons as he had, what a great help they could be to one another. Darek had noticed that food was not plentiful in the valley. Maybe that was why there were so few dragons left. The Zorians were great farmers. They could grow food for the dragons, and in return the dragons could help the Zorians in many ways. They could light fires. They could help plow the fields with their great claws. And *then*, there was the flying! Even a small dragon could probably carry four Zorians in its pouch at once. Journeys of several days could be made in hours! Darek could hardly wait to tell everyone of his discovery. He would probably become famous, maybe even go down in history. . . .

Darek finally fell asleep, dreaming of a bright new future for dragons and Zorians alike.

* * *

"*Grrrawk!*" Darek woke with a start. The Great Blue had jumped up and rushed, roaring, to the mouth of the cave. Darek scrambled to his feet. He edged along the side of the cave and peeked out. There on a ledge just below the cave were his father, Clep, and the full Zorian hunting party.

The Great Blue roared again, head up, flames shooting out. Dragons began to emerge from the other caves. The Zorians formed a battle circle, shields and weapons pointing out. Darek's father, Clep, and several other men aimed up at the Great Blue.

"Father, no!" Darek shrieked. He ran out beneath the Great Blue's legs and waved his arms.

"Darek!" yelled his father. "Are you all right?"

"I'm fine," Darek shouted. He looked up at the Great Blue. "Wait, please!" he yelled to her. "Let me talk to them."

The Blue reared and tossed her head from side to side. Darek turned back to the hunters. "Lower your weapons," he shouted. "You're making her nervous."

No one made any move to obey.

"Move aside, son," Darek's father called firmly.

"You don't understand," Darek insisted. "They're peaceful. They only fight to defend themselves. They're not the same as the dragons in the old days. They don't even eat flesh!"

Darek's words seemed to bounce off his father's stony face. "*Get out of the way, son!*" he repeated.

Darek turned to Clep. "Clep, you've got to make him listen," he begged.

Clep lowered his bow slightly and glanced uneasily at his father. "Maybe he's telling the truth," Darek heard him say. "Maybe we should listen."

"He is a child!" Darek's father yelled. "What does he know of dragons? Raise your bow!"

Clep raised his bow again, but when he looked up at Darek he seemed torn.

"Please!" Darek shouted again. "I *do* speak the truth." No one but Clep paid him any heed. Even Yoran's father, Bodak, turned a deaf ear to his pleas.

"*Grrrawk! Grrrawk!*" The Great Blue reared back. Flames shot out of her mouth.

"*For the last time,*" Darek's father yelled, "*get out of the way!*"

Darek stood trembling before his father's icy stare. All his life he had wanted nothing more than to make his father proud. Now he stood defying him. Why? Zantor bumped Darek's arm and whimpered. Darek looked down into the dragonling's gentle face and knew why. If killing without cause was what it took to be a man, he wanted no part of it.

The Great Blue roared and lifted her head. Darek saw his father narrow his eyes and train his bow on the dragon. "*Ready!*" he yelled. "*Aim!*"

Darek put his arms around Zantor and closed his eyes.

9

"*Stop!*"

The scream that split the air was piercing enough to be heard above the dragons.

Darek opened his eyes and stared. There, on the ridge beside the twin rocks, stood his mother. Zilah, Yoran's mother, was with her, and so were most of the other village women.

"Mother!" Darek called out.

Darek's father roared. "Are you mad, woman? Get back, or the dragons will tear you to pieces!"

Darek watched, amazed, as his mother and the other women ignored his father's warning and began the dangerous climb toward the cave. The dragons, too, seemed stunned. Even the Great Blue stopped her roaring and thrashing and stood watching.

Darek glanced anxiously at the dragons as his mother and the others struggled for footings. Should the dragons decide to attack, they would be easy pickings.

"Get back, I tell you!" Darek's father repeated, but the women came on. At last Darek's mother reached the mouth of the cave, and Darek rushed into her arms. She hugged him tight, then looked uneasily up at the Great Blue.

"She won't hurt us," Darek said. "She's only protecting her babies."

Darek's mother nodded. She held up her hands. "I have no weapons," she told the Great Blue. Then she folded her arms around Darek again. "I am a mother, like you."

The Great Blue seemed to understand. She nudged Zantor back into the shadows.

"Take the boy and get out of there," Darek's father yelled, "while you've still got the chance!"

Darek's mother stepped to the ledge.

"It is not the dragons I fear," she shouted. "It is you."

Darek stared at his mother. Never in his life had he seen her speak so to his father. The other men stared too, and Darek's father's face grew as red as a burning ember.

"Perhaps I should leave you with the dragons then?" he shouted.

The other women came up and stood behind Darek's mother.

"You will have to leave us all," she said. "We stand together. No longer will we let our sons be slaughtered for this cruel sport."

An angry murmur passed through the men and Darek's father's eyes burned with rage. "*Sport!*" he shouted. "You call it *sport* to defend our people from their enemies?"

Darek's mother looked around at the great dragons on the cliffs. "If these creatures were truly our enemies," she said, "would I be standing unharmed before you now?"

Some of the men began to glance uncomfortably at one another.

"The old days are gone," Darek's mother went on. "We have suffered enough pain. Look at what you have done to Zilah. And to Marla and Deela and all the others whose sons are gone." Darek's mother pulled Darek close and her voice began to tremble. "Look at what you would have done to me today."

Suddenly there was a cry, and Bodak, Yoran's father, dropped to his knees. He put his hands over his face and his shoulders began to shake. He was weeping, Darek realized. A hard lump formed in his throat. He had never seen a man weep before.

There was a moment of stunned and awkward silence, and then, one by one, the men began to lower their weapons.

10

Darek stood by the entrance to the cave. A few ashes were all that remained of the pile of weapons. The dragons were still cautious, but they had allowed the villagers to return safely to the twin rocks. Darek was sure that friendship would come in time. He turned to Zantor. A great sadness filled his heart.

"You've grown already, little friend," he said. "Soon you *will* be the greatest Great Blue of them all."

Zantor thrummed happily.

"You stay with your new mother now," Darek said, "and maybe we'll see each other again some day." Darek started toward the twin rocks. Zantor scuffled after him.

"No," said Darek firmly. "You have to stay."

Zantor stopped obediently and stood watching until Darek reached the ridge. "*Rrronk?*" he cried out.

Darek looked back and waved, then he turned and hurried forward, blinking back tears. Just as he reached the group there was a flutter and a thump, and then Zantor rushed up from behind and stuffed his head under Darek's shirt. "*Thrrummm, thrrummm, thrrummm,*" he said.

Darek giggled and pushed the dragonling away. "Will you cut that out?" he said.

The villagers laughed.

"Looks like you've adopted yourself a dragon," said Zilah.

Darek's father snorted. "No son of mine is going to play nursemaid to any dragon!"

Darek looked at Zantor. Clearly the dragonling wanted to come home with him, and Darek wanted nothing more. If only he could convince his father.

"Father . . . ?" he began.

His father eyed him suspiciously.

"I was thinking," Darek went on, his stomach fluttering, "the dragons could be our friends. They can light cook fires, they can help plow, they can even take us flying. I flew in the Great Blue's pouch. It was *wonderful!*"

In his growing excitement Darek did not notice his father's eyes growing rounder, and his face growing redder.

"*Enough!*" he boomed. "By the twin moons of Zoriak! What madness will you dream up next?" He whirled and stormed away.

Darek stared after him, his heart as heavy

as stone. His mother put a hand on his shoulder and smiled.

"Change is never easy, my son," she said. "Your father has come a long way today. Give him time."

Zilah and Bodak stood nearby. Darek saw Zilah press Bodak's arm and whisper something into his ear. They murmured together, then Bodak nodded gravely.

"Your words are not easy to accept, young Darek," he said, "but they have much wisdom. Bring the orphan along. Zilah and I will care for him until your father is ready to listen."

Darek's heart leaped with joy, but he bowed his head humbly. "Thank you, Bodak," he said. "You honor me."

"And *I* honor my brother as well."

Darek looked up. Clep was standing before him, holding out the dragonclaw necklace. "This belongs to you," he said.

Darek was confused. "But why?" he asked. "You earned it."

Clep shook his head. "I just got lucky," he said. "It took true courage to do what you did today."

Darek's heart swelled with pride at Clep's praise. He took the prize and held it up. Somehow it brought him no joy now. He heard Zantor whimper beside him. Slowly he lowered his hand again. How could he return the gift to Clep without appearing ungrateful?

Clep seemed to understand. "Perhaps," he said quietly, "it really belongs to the dragons."

Together Darek and Clep dug a hole and buried the necklace between the twin rocks. Then they stood for a moment, side by side, looking out over the valley, peaceful and still now in the late afternoon shadows. Zantor wiggled in between them.

"*Thrrummm, thrrummm, thrrummm,*" he said.

A Dragon
in the Family

For Bobby,
who fights a Red-Fanged Dragon
with a sword made of courage
and a shield made of love

1

Darek sat across the campfire from his father, chewing but not tasting his food. It had been three days since their confrontation in the Valley of the Dragons, and still his father had hardly said a word to him. Would it be any different when they and the rest of their party reached home tomorrow? He glanced at his mother and his brother, Clep, and they each gave him a small, reassuring smile. Change takes time, his mother kept telling him. How much time? Darek wondered. He longed for the day when his father would gaze upon him with love and pride again.

"*Rrronk,*" came a sad cry from back in the shadows.

Darek's father looked up from his meal and frowned.

"I'll quiet him," said Darek, jumping up. He lit a torch and picked his way through the forest to the spot where the dragonling had been tied. He saw the green eyes shining in the night before he could make out the small form huddled beneath a zarnrod tree.

"*Rrronk, rrronk,*" came the cry again.

"It's all right, Zantor," Darek called softly.

"*Thrummm,*" the creature sang happily when it heard Darek's voice. It strained against the chain that held it fast.

Darek stuck his torch in the ground and quickly unlocked the collar. The soft blue scales underneath were torn and the flesh was rubbed raw from the dragonling's efforts to free itself.

"I'm sorry, Zantor," Darek whispered, stroking the small, bony head. "This is Father's idea. He still finds it hard to trust you, though I keep telling him you're no threat to the yukes or anything else."

Zantor nuzzled Darek and Darek smiled. "Come, little friend," he whispered. "Let's find you some supper."

Darek lifted the torch and led the way down the path as the creature fluttered and danced around him, happy to be free. They came upon a patch of barliberry bushes, and Darek sat on a rock and watched while Zantor fed hungrily.

Darek still had to pinch himself sometimes, so strange did it seem to be friends with a dragon. He remembered how startled he had been that night, after the last dragonquest, when he had found the newborn in its dead mother's pouch. He hadn't known what to do. Watching the little dragon now, though, Darek knew he had made the right decision.

Returning Zantor to the Valley of the Dragons had led Darek to an important discovery. The dragons, which he had been taught to hate and fear all his life, were not what they appeared to be. Fierce only when threatened, they wanted nothing more than to be left alone to live in peace.

When Darek had shared this news with the members of the search party who came after him, the women had welcomed it — no more of their sons would have to die in the ritual dragonquests. But the men were harder to convince. It had taken Bodak, whose son, Yoran, had died in the last dragonquest, to turn the tide.

Zantor shuffled over and dropped a cluster of barliberries in Darek's lap. Darek smiled and scratched the little dragon under its chin.

"I still can't believe Father is letting you come home with us," Darek whispered. "But then, how could he object when Bodak and Zilah offered to take you in, even knowing that your mother killed their son?"

The dragonling snuggled down against Darek's leg, and Darek pulled a berry from the clump in his lap and chewed it thoughtfully. Why was Father still angry? he wondered. The other villagers in their party seemed to see the value of befriending the dragons. There would be no more fighting, no more killing. The dragons and Zorians could help one another in many ways. Most exciting of all, the dragons could take the Zorians flying! Darek's eyes shone as he remembered his own flight in the pouch of a Great Blue.

Then, as quickly as it had come, his joy faded into worry again. Darek's father was Chief Marksman, an important man in the village, soon to join the Circle of Elders. What if the Elders felt as he did? What if they accused Darek of treason? Treason was a serious crime.

Crime! Darek suddenly sat up straight,

eyes wide, heart thumping. No wonder his father was so upset. Now Darek understood. Darek had been so preoccupied by the dragonling, he hadn't stopped to think that he might be committing a crime. In Zoriak, if a child under the age of twelve committed a crime, it was the father who suffered the punishment! And Darek was only nine. A heavy weight settled in his chest. Much as he loved the little dragon, he loved his father more. The last thing he wanted was to get him in trouble.

Darek heard a soft "*flubba bub bub bub, flubba bub bub bub*." He looked down to see the dragon curled up, gently snoring, his chin resting on Darek's foot. Darek sighed. His heart felt like the rope in a tug-of-war, pulled first this way, then that, until it was ready to snap.

"Why did my brother have to kill your mother?" he whispered to the sleeping dragon. "Why did your mother have to kill Yoran?"

"*Flubba bub bub bub*" was the dragon's only response, but Darek stared up at the night sky and found his answer in the cold and silent stars. The killings had happened because the killings had always happened, and unless Darek could make a change, the killings would go on and on and on . . .

2

Darek could hear the village bell clanging while he and the others were still some distance from town. The lookout had obviously caught sight of them. By the time they reached the bottom of the mountain pass, the village square was filled with people.

"Hooray!" the villagers shouted when they caught sight of Darek. "The boy has been found. The boy is well!" Then, on the heels of their cheers came another sound. A gasp of surprise swept through the crowd. "A drag-onling!" Darek heard. "There's a dragon with him!"

Darek pulled in Zantor's chain, keeping him close. The crowd and the noise were making the creature skittish, and Darek wanted no problems. His father was already upset enough, staring straight ahead, stony faced as he strode along beside Darek. What was going through his father's mind? Darek wondered. What fate awaited them all?

"Darek! Darek!"

Darek whirled at the sound of the familiar voice. "Pola? Pola, where are you?" Darek searched for his best friend in the sea of faces around him.

"Here. Over here." A hand waved fran-tically, then Pola burst through the crowd and rushed up and threw his arms around Darek. "You're safe!" he cried.

"Yes, yes, I'm fine . . ."

"What happened? They say you went to the Valley of the Dragons. They say —"

Suddenly Pola stopped talking and pulled back. He stared oddly at Darek. "By the twin moons of Zoriak," he whispered, "what happened to you?" He pointed at Darek's belly.

Darek looked down. In his excitement over seeing his friend he hadn't noticed that Zantor had somehow wiggled in between them and shoved his head up under Darek's tunic, making Darek look like a four-legged, blue-tailed beast that was about to deliver a baby.

Darek laughed in spite of his fear. "Will you get out of there," he whispered, pushing Zantor's head down and out.

"*Rrronk!*" cried the little beast. He ducked between Darek's legs and shoved his head up under the back side of the tunic.

Darek grinned, red faced, at Pola. "It's — it's a dragon," he stammered. "He — uh — thinks I'm his mother."

"A what?!" Pola took another step back.

"It's okay," Darek hurried to say. "He's harmless. See?" He gently pushed the dragon out from under his tunic again and coaxed it around front. "That's a good boy," he murmured, rubbing the knobby head affectionately.

"DAREK!" Darek jumped and the dragonling dived between his legs and up under his tunic again. Darek turned in the direction of his father's voice and saw that the crowd had parted to let Yanek pass. His father and the Chief Elder waited up ahead in the village square. "Bring the beast forward," his father yelled.

Darek gulped. "I gotta go," he whispered nervously to Pola. "I'll explain later." He hurried forward, dragging the baby dragon along behind.

3

Darek stared up into the stern eyes of the Chief Elder and blurted out the whole story — how he had found the newborn dragon and taken it back to the Valley of the Dragons, how a Great Blue Dragon had befriended them, and finally, how he had placed himself between the dragons and the Zorian rescue party in order to avert a battle.

"The dragons let us go unharmed," Darek ended breathlessly. "Don't you see? They didn't want to fight. They don't like to fight. They only fight to protect their young."

The Chief Elder's hard expression never wavered. If he found any of this news surprising, he gave no sign. All around them the villagers crowded close, murmuring in hushed tones and waiting for the Chief's reaction. Overhead the violet rays of the Zorian sun beat down. Beads of sweat began to trickle down Darek's neck and back.

Suddenly Darek felt something tickle between his shoulder blades. He twitched and tried to ignore it, but it came again. Zantor, still hiding under the back of Darek's tunic, was licking the droplets of salty sweat with his scratchy tongue. Darek twitched again and tried to hold back a giggle, but it was no use. The more he twitched, the more the little tongue flicked. At last Darek could stand it no more. He burst out laughing and crumpled up in a heap of hysterics, rolling and kicking on the ground, trying to get away from the tickly tongue. The more Darek laughed, though, the more Zantor seemed to think it was all a great game, and no sooner would Darek roll free than the little beast would pounce again, seeking out another bare patch of skin to tease. Round and round in the dust they rolled, laughing and thrumming, wiggling and tickling until at last they both lay still, too exhausted to move another muscle.

Darek lay on his stomach in the dirt, still giggling in little bursts and trying to catch his breath when he noticed the sea of boots and clogs around him.

"Uh oh," he mumbled, remembering where he was and why. He slowly rolled over and looked up.

The Chief Elder's eyes were hard as granite, and Darek's father's face was crimson, but, Darek noted with some relief, many of the other villagers were smiling.

"Rise!" the Chief's voice boomed.

Darek scrambled to his feet and the dragon darted behind him and dived under his shirt again. The Chief Elder's face wrinkled in disgust. He turned to a pair of guards who stood nearby.

"Take the beast to the guardhouse," he said.

"The guardhouse!" Darek cried, his arms shielding the dragon. "No, you can't!"

The Chief Elder nodded to the guards and they began to circle Darek.

"No. Please," Darek argued, circling too, trying to keep his body between the dragonling and the guards. "You don't understand. He'll be terrified."

One of the guards lunged and grabbed Zantor by the tail.

"*Rrronk! Rrronk!*" the dragonling yowled, digging his claws into Darek's back.

"Ouch! Stop! Please! He's clawing me! Aaagh!"

The guard went on pulling, the dragon went on clawing, and Darek went on screaming until at last Darek heard his mother yell, "Yanek, for the sake of Lord Eternal, do something!"

Darek's father finally stepped forward and gave the guard a shove that sent him sprawling backward into the dust. Gasps of surprise rippled through the crowd, but Darek hardly noticed, intent on freeing himself from Zantor's frantic clutches. At last he coaxed the dragonling out from under his tunic.

"It's okay, Zantor. It's okay," he whispered. "I won't let them take you away." Zantor shivered and nuzzled his head against Darek's chest.

Darek's father went over and extended a hand to help the fallen guard to his feet, then he turned, his face crimson again, and bowed to the Chief Elder.

"A thousand pardons, Sire . . ." he began.

"Silence!" The Chief Elder gestured to the guards. "Throw him in the guardhouse too!" he bellowed.

The guards grabbed hold of Darek's father, but before they could take him away Darek's mother rushed up and linked arms with her husband. Bodak and his wife, Zilah, quickly joined them, then another woman and another man. Soon the whole rescue party stood arm in arm. Darek's father seemed startled, and deeply touched.

"Sire," he said, his voice stronger now, "my son speaks the truth. Those of us who followed him to the Valley of the Dragons have seen it for ourselves. The time has come to talk."

4

An immediate meeting of the Circle of Elders was called. Darek's father and Bodak were commanded to attend.

"What do you think will happen?" Darek and his brother, Clep, asked their mother as they made their way home, trailed very closely by Zantor.

"I don't know," she said simply. "We'll just have to wait and see."

"But can't we do something in the meantime?" Darek begged.

"Yes," said his mother. "We can do the chores. Lord Eternal knows they've been left waiting long enough."

Zantor stepped on Darek's heel. Darek staggered a few feet, then regained his balance. He turned and glared down at the dragonling, who bumped smack into him again in his haste to catch up. All this togetherness was beginning to get on Darek's nerves. "Is it necessary to walk on my feet?" he snapped.

The little dragon stared up at him a moment in surprise, then — *thwip!* — out darted the forked tongue, planting a tickly little dragon kiss right on Darek's lips.

Darek rolled his eyes skyward, and Clep and their mother burst out laughing. Darek couldn't help laughing too, which made Zantor do a happy little shuffling jig.

"That's the way," said Darek, nodding to the dragon. "Practice being cute. You're going to need all your tricks when Father comes back and finds we've brought you home with us."

"Well," said Darek's mother, "I don't see what choice we had, other than sending you off to live with Bodak and Zilah too."

Darek's smile faded and he sighed. "I fear Father will think that the better choice," he said.

Darek's mother slid an arm around his shoulders as they walked. "Don't you believe that," she said. "Not for a moment. Your father may be worried and confused, but he still loves you very much."

"Enough to put up with a dragon in the family?" asked Darek.

Darek's mother reached over and patted the little horn nubs on Zantor's head. "Yes," she said, "I think so . . . in time."

"In time?" Darek frowned. "But what are we to do *now?* Father will be back in a little while."

They had reached home, and Darek's mother pushed open the garden gate and looked over at the messy, neglected barnyard. "I think chores would be a *very* good idea," she said.

5

Fortunately, most of the yukes had new calves, so they had not suffered for lack of milking. The zok eggs had piled up some, though, and were beginning to smell. The zoks squawked and scolded as Darek and Clep reached into their nests and gathered up the eggs.

"*Rrronk, rrronk,*" cried Zantor when the boys carried two brimming basketfuls of foul-smelling eggs out of the zok house. They carried them down near the river, then went to get shovels. But by the time they returned, Zantor had already dug a deep hole and pushed the eggs in. As the boys watched, he neatly covered the hole over again.

"Wow," said Clep. "He's pretty handy to have around."

"I told you," said Darek. "Imagine the things a big one could do. It could plow up a field in no time!"

"Yeah," said Clep thoughtfully. "Or dig irrigation ditches."

"Or help in the zitanium mines," added Darek.

"Or dig a swimming hole," said Clep, eyes shining. Darek and Clep had always dreamed of having their own swimming hole.

"Sure," said Darek as they picked up their shovels and headed back to the paddock. "All we'd have to do is feed them."

"Feed them!" Clep wrinkled up his brow. "Did you happen to notice how big they get?"

"Of course I did. But with all their help we could easily raise enough food."

Clep still looked skeptical.

"Wanna see something else?" said Darek. He picked up a couple of sticks and placed them on the ground. Immediately Zantor started shuffling around and nudging more sticks into the pile. When the pile was just the right size for a campfire — *whoosh!* — a stream of flame shot out of the little dragon's mouth and set it all ablaze.

"Wow," Clep repeated.

"That's nothing," said Darek, and he launched into the story of how he had flown in the pouch of a Great Blue, high above the Valley of the Dragons. Darek had already told Clep the story, several times in fact, on the journey back from the Valley, but Darek could see that Clep was only just now beginning to believe it. Darek smiled, thinking how hard it would be for him to believe if it hadn't actually happened to him.

"It's like nothing you've done in your life before, Clep," he said wistfully. "They are the most magnificent creatures!"

Clep stared at Darek a moment, then looked away.

"What's wrong?" asked Darek.

"Nothing," said Clep.

"Yes there is. I can see it. Tell me, Clep. Please."

Clep kicked another stick into the fire and shoved his hands into his breeches. "It's just that . . . well, a couple of days ago I was a hero, a Marksman. Now I feel like a murderer. You've changed everything, Darek. I don't know what I am anymore."

SPLAT!

A zok egg came flying over the paddock wall and hit Darek square in the middle of the forehead.

SPLAT! SPLAT! A shower of rotten, rank-smelling zok eggs followed, pelting Darek, Clep, and Zantor.

"Traitors!" they heard. "Dragon lovers!"

Darek and Clep tried to protect themselves, but the eggs were coming too fast. The

sticky yolks dripped in their eyes and blinded them. The smell made them gag. Then there was another sound, something between a "*Rrronk*" and "*Grrrawk,*" followed by frightened yells and running footsteps, and the egg shower stopped.

Darek wiped the egg from his eyes and stared. Zantor was perched atop the paddock wall, wings spread, claws unsheathed, flames shooting from his mouth in a full dragon battle stance.

Darek and Clep raced to the wall in time to see a gang of young Zorian boys retreating over the nearest hill.

"Wow," said Clep, staring up at Zantor in awe. "I didn't think he had it in him. Did you ever see him act like that?"

Darek didn't answer. He was still staring at the hill.

"Darek," said Clep, "what's wrong?"

"I saw one of them," said Darek quietly. "It was Pola."

6

_____

"Try to understand," said Clep. "I probably would have done the same thing a week ago. The truth is, so would you."

Darek scrubbed the last of the rotten egg from his face, then bent down and ducked his head under the water again. Clep was right, he knew. Zorian boys spent years training for their dragonquests. If someone had tried to tell him just last week that everything had changed, that he would never get to go on his, he would have been furious. He waded in toward the riverbank, shaking the water from his hair. Clep tossed him a drying cloth.

"Maybe you're right," Darek admitted, "but I never would have done anything like this to Pola. Never. He didn't even let me explain."

"Maybe it wasn't him," said Clep. "Maybe it was just somebody who looks like him from the back."

"Yeah," said Darek. "Maybe you're right." It made him feel better to believe that, even if it wasn't the truth.

Zantor still frolicked in the river, and the two brothers stood on the bank and watched him for a moment, deep in thought.

"It's all going wrong," said Darek quietly. "I thought everyone would be happy. I thought it would be so easy."

"I knew it wouldn't be easy," said Clep, "but it's the right thing to do."

Darek looked up at his big brother in

surprise. "Do you really believe that?" he asked.

Clep nodded and clapped Darek on the shoulder. "Yes, I do." He smiled at his little brother's astonishment. "I even heard Bodak tell Father that he thinks you have the makings of a great leader."

"Bodak said that?"

Clep nodded and Darek thought quietly for a moment. "What answer did Father make?" he asked.

Clep avoided his eyes. "There's the dinner bell!" he said quickly, seeming glad of a reason to change the subject. "Hurry and get dressed now."

Darek and Clep closed Zantor up in the barn with a pile of barliberries and a promise to return quickly, and to their surprise, he did not protest. He seemed to sense that this was home now. When they got to the kitchen, their father was already there. His face was grim and Darek's heart squeezed with fear. He longed to ask what had happened at the Circle, but his voice would not come out.

Clep started to ask, but a glance from their mother silenced him.

"Let your father have dinner," she said, "then we'll talk."

They ate in silence, Darek and Clep stealing worried glances at each other and at their father's somber face. At last Yanek pushed his plate away and lit his pipe. He sucked in deeply, then blew a long column of smoke from his lips.

"Is the beast with Zilah?" he asked.

Darek glanced nervously at Clep and their mother. "N-no," he stammered. "He wouldn't go with her. He's in the barn."

Darek's father nodded tiredly as if he'd expected as much, then went on smoking his pipe in silence. At last Darek couldn't stand the suspense any longer.

"What did the Circle decide?" he blurted out. "What was the vote?"

Darek's father took the pipe from his lips. "The Circle voted to put the beast to death," he said.

A cry of protest sprang instantly to Darek's lips, but his father held up a finger for silence. "I'm not through," he chided.

Darek nodded obediently and his father went on.

"Bodak and I convinced the Circle that the beast deserves a trial," he said.

Darek's eyes opened wide in wonder. "You did?"

"Yes."

"But . . . why would you? I mean, I thought you didn't . . ."

Darek's father took another long puff on his pipe. "I'm a fair man," he said, then smiled at his wife and added, "if not always the most flexible one."

Darek's mother reached over and squeezed

her husband's hand. "True on both counts," she said with a wink at Darek.

The great weight of the past few days began to lift from Darek's heart, but Clep still looked worried.

"What manner of trial do the elders have in mind?" he asked.

"Simply this," Yanek answered. "The beast can live among us until the first sign of trouble."

"And if there *is* trouble?" Clep inquired.

Darek's father glanced at the faces of his wife and sons, then lowered his eyes. "*Then* he will be put to death," he said quietly, "and so will Bodak and I."

7

Darek sat on a bale of zorgrass watching Zantor try to perch on a yuke stall like a zok. It was obvious that the dragonling was doing his best to make Darek laugh, but Darek's heart was too heavy. How could this be happening? he wondered. How could an act of love and caring get twisted into such a nightmare?

"It isn't fair," he cried out. "It just isn't fair!"

"What isn't fair?"

Darek turned and saw his father standing in the doorway. Darek turned away again, fighting with all his might to hold back the tears. "Nothing," he said softly.

There were footsteps and then Darek felt a hand on his shoulder.

"Mind if I sit down?"

Darek looked up, and then the tears stung his eyes and slid down his cheeks. "Oh, Father," he whispered. "I'm so sorry."

Darek's father sat down next to him, leaned his elbows on his knees, and clasped his hands together tightly.

"No, son," he said. "I am the one who is sorry."

"You?" Darek started to protest, but Yanek held up a finger to silence him.

"Hear me," he commanded.

Darek wiped his eyes and nodded.

"I have treated you badly," Yanek went on. "In truth, the anger I have shown to you

these past few days was really anger and con-tempt for myself."

Darek stared at his father in astonishment. "But why?" he asked.

Yanek rubbed his forehead tiredly. "Because in my heart I have known for a long time the truth about the dragons, and I have denied it."

Darek's mouth fell open in disbelief, and Yanek shook his head as if irritated with himself. "In the old days," he went on, "when the Red-Fanged and Purple-Spiked Dragons roamed the Valley, our fathers were great warriors. Their skills protected their families. Their deeds of valor gave them places of honor in our society. They fought until the Reds and Purples were gone."

Yanek fell silent and Darek stared at him in confusion. "Then what happened?" he asked.

Darek's father sighed. "What is a warrior without a war?" he asked. "Somehow all dragons became the enemy. Green-Horned, Yellow-Crested, Great Blue . . . what matter that their kind never bothered our villages? What matter that they had not even a taste for flesh? When a man wants to be a hero he needs a foe to vanquish."

Darek looked over at Zantor, who had finally accomplished the task he had set for himself and sat staring at them proudly like an oversize blue zok. The sight was so comical that Darek might have laughed if he hadn't felt so heartsick.

"Then it's all been a lie," he said. "All the training, all the battles, all the deaths . . ."

Yanek nodded slowly. "Yes," he said, "and that's why what you have done is so dangerous."

"Dangerous?" Darek repeated.

"Yes," said his father. "I'm afraid our whole society is built around this lie, and those who have gained the most from it will fight hardest to keep the truth a secret."

"You mean . . . the Circle of Elders," said Darek.

"Yes," said Yanek.

"But how?" asked Darek. "How can they fight this?"

"The same way they always have, my son. By making the lie appear to be true, so true that they can believe it themselves."

"How can they do that?"

There was a sudden commotion out in the yard, followed by the sound of many voices raised in anger.

Darek's father stiffened. "I fear we are about to see how," he whispered.

"Yanek!" a voice boomed. "Yanek of Zoriak, come forth!"

8

Darek's father was grabbed by a guard as soon as he and Darek emerged from the barn. His arms were shackled behind his back and he was pushed over to where Bodak stood, shackled as well. A great crowd of villagers had assembled into the paddock and the Circle of Elders stood at its center.

"What's wrong?" Darek cried. "What are you going to do with my father?"

"Silence!" the Chief Elder boomed. "Where are you hiding the beast?"

"The beast?" said Darek, so frightened that for a moment he couldn't think what the Chief Elder meant.

"Don't play the fool!" the Chief bellowed. "We know . . ."

He never had to finish his sentence, for at that moment a zok strutted out of the barn, and right behind it strutted Zantor, doing the silliest zok imitation Darek had ever seen.

No one was amused.

"He's there!" came a panicky cry. "Watch out! Seize him!"

Shrieks of fear rang out on all sides, and before Darek knew what was happening, Zantor was snagged in a chain-mail net. A zitanium cage was rolled up and the little creature was tossed inside.

"*Rrronk! Rrronk!*" he cried out.

Now that the dragonling was safely locked up, a group of children began to tease and taunt him, poking him with sticks and tossing stones into the cage. Zantor's "*rrronks!*"

became shrill "*grrrawks!*" He unsheathed his claws and began charging at the bars, arrows of flame shooting from his mouth.

"Do you see?" screamed a hysterical mother to the elders. "Is it not as I said?"

The Chief Elder nodded slowly. His face was stern, but it was obvious that he was well pleased with the events that were taking place before him.

At that moment Darek's mother burst out of the house, followed by Clep.

"What's going on?" she cried, staring wildly at the scene before her. "What's happened?"

"I fear, Madam," said the Chief Elder, "that the beast has attacked a group of boys unprovoked. Friends of your son, I believe."

Darek's eyes widened. "That's a lie!" he shouted.

"A lie?" The Chief Elder turned toward Darek. He smiled slowly and snapped his fingers. "Bring the boys here," he called over his

shoulder. Two mothers came forward with two boys Darek knew, but not well.

"See for yourself," said the Chief.

The boys turned and Darek saw that their clothes were scorched and their hair singed. The chief gave Darek a smug look.

"They're not friends!" Darek cried. "They tried to hurt me and Clep. Zantor was just defending us."

The Chief turned a deaf ear to Darek's pleas. "Take the prisoners to the council house!" he shouted. "Let the trials begin!"

9

Darek stared helplessly as Zantor continued to thrash and roar in his cage outside the council house. Now and then the dragonling made a new sound, an earsplitting "*Eeeiiieee!*" If found guilty, Zantor would be the lucky one, though. He would simply be target practice for the archers. Darek's father and Bodak would be burned at the stake.

Darek's mother and Zilah tried desperately to convince the waiting villagers that Zantor,

Yanek, and Bodak were innocent, but the group of boys continued to hold to their story of terror, and sympathy was on their side.

Darek and Clep paced nervously.

"I've got to *do* something," said Darek. "I can't just wait here like this."

"Haven't you done enough already?" Clep snapped.

Darek stopped pacing and stared at his brother. "Are you blaming me, Clep?" he asked quietly.

"Yes . . . No." Clep put his hands over his face. "I don't know what to think anymore. I just want it to be a bad dream. I want to wake up and find out that it's just an ordinary day and we're all going fishing like we used to, me and Yoran, and you and Pola —"

"Pola!" Darek grabbed Clep by the shoulders and stared into his eyes. "Pola was with them, remember? Pola knows the truth!"

Clep stared back for a moment, then shook

his head. "You're not sure of that," he said, "and even if he was with them, what makes you think he'll tell the truth?"

Darek stared over Clep's shoulder at Zantor. "He'll tell," he whispered. "I'll *make* him tell."

Darek found Pola out behind his house, shooting arrows aimlessly into the air.

"Pola!" he shouted. "Pola, we've got to talk!"

Pola glanced over his shoulder at Darek, frowned, and looked away again. He loosed another arrow, watching its lazy flight.

"Pola, listen to me!" Darek ran up behind his friend, grabbed his arm, and whirled him around.

"Hey," Pola growled, pulling his arm free. "Leave me alone."

"No!" Darek shouted. "You've got to help me."

"Help you do what?" asked Pola sullenly.

Darek stared at him. "Haven't you heard?" he asked. "Don't you know?"

"Know what?" asked Pola.

"They're trying my father," shouted Darek, "and my friend Zantor." Darek narrowed his eyes. "You know," he added dryly, "the fierce dragon who attacks young boys unprovoked."

Pola's eyes widened, then he looked away.

"I — I don't know what you're talking about," he said.

"No?" Darek grabbed the hat from Pola's head and clutched a handful of singed hair. "Then how did you get this?"

Pola said nothing.

"Answer me, Pola!"

"I — I never meant to hurt your father," mumbled Pola. "I just wanted to get the dragon."

Darek let go of Pola's hair and handed him his hat. "Why?" he asked angrily. "What did the dragon do to you?"

Pola whirled away and slammed his bow to the ground.

"It doesn't belong here!" he shouted. "It changes everything, don't you see? All the training, the matches, the tournaments, all the games of skill we've played all our lives! None of them matter anymore."

Darek stared at the bow lying between them on the ground. He wanted to hate Pola, but he couldn't. He understood Pola's feelings too well. In his heart he knew he would have felt the same way once.

A great clamor of voices rose up, carried on the wind from the village square. Time was running out. Darek had to win Pola to his side now. He grabbed up the bow and found an arrow that lay nearby. He fitted the arrow to the string and surveyed the meadow. Far away on the opposite side stood a young purple sapling. Reaching it would be quite a stretch, but Darek had to try. He tilted the bow up and let fly. He

watched, holding his breath as the arrow arched out high over the meadow, then dropped slowly and . . . struck! Praise Lord Eternal. His aim was true.

Darek lowered the bow and looked at Pola. His friend was envious of the shot, he could tell. "Here," he said, holding out the bow. "Match that."

"What?"

"Match it," Darek repeated.

"Why?" asked Pola, narrowing his eyes.

"Because you want to," said Darek. "Admit it. Whether you ever fight a dragon or not, you *want* to shoot, because you want to prove you're as good as me. That's where the fun lies, Pola. In the competition, not the killing. Match it. I dare you."

Pola stared at Darek a long time, then silently took the bow and pulled an arrow from his quiver. Slowly he turned, fitted the arrow to the string, and took aim. Darek held his breath again as the arrow arched out over the meadow, going higher, higher, then lower, lower, and . . .

"Yah!" shrieked Pola, tossing his hat into the air.

The boys clutched each other in a brother-hood hug as their arrows quivered side by side far across the meadow.

10
_____

Darek was prepared for a guilty verdict, but he was not prepared for the sight that greeted him when he and Pola reached the square. The executions had begun! Yanek and Bodak were lashed to their stakes, and archers were lining up in front of Zantor's cage.

"Stop!" Darek shrieked as he and Pola tried to push their way through the crowd. "Stop! It's all a mistake!"

No one listened. No one cared. Everyone

was too busy watching the show, shouting and jeering.

"Stop!" the two boys cried together. "Somebody listen, please!" Darek pushed and shoved at the crowd, but he was making no headway. He pushed at a big man who pushed him back and sent him sprawling in the dust. Darek scrambled to his feet again, grabbed a rock, and motioned Pola to follow. He got as close as he could to the platform where the village bell sat, then let the rock fly.

CLANG . . . ANG . . . ANG!

All heads turned as Darek hoisted himself up onto the platform and pulled Pola up too.

"Stop!" he yelled. "This is all a mistake! We've got to stop the executions now!"

The Chief Elder gave a signal, and the guards touched flaming torches to the piles of brush that circled Yanek and Bodak.

"NO!" Darek cried. "These men are innocent!"

"It's true," Pola shouted. "I was among the

boys." He turned so people could see his singed hair, then turned back and hung his head in shame. "We attacked Darek and Clep," he went on. "We provoked the beast!"

Mouths dropped open and a hush fell over the crowd. Then, "He's lying!" someone shouted.

"Aye! Aye!"

"No!" Pola cried. "It's the truth." He scanned the crowd before him. "Malek!" he said suddenly. "Dorwin!" He pointed to the two boys who had brought the charges. "Tell them! This has gone too far."

All eyes turned toward the two boys. They stared at each other uncomfortably for a moment, then slowly nodded and hung their heads. The crowd gasped.

"Don't you see?" shouted Darek. "The only lie is that the dragons are our enemies! Do they attack our villages? Do they raid our herds? No! They fight only when we attack them, only when they are provoked!"

Darek could see that he had the attention of the crowd now. He pointed to where his mother and Zilah stood. "Zilah's son is dead," he said, "and so is my mother's brother. How many others of you have lost sons, brothers, husbands, or fathers?"

People murmured together, then a hand went up, followed by another, and another. Darek watched until almost everyone had a hand in the air. "Look!" he shouted. "Turn your heads and *look,* and then decide. . . . How many more must die for the sake of a lie?"

Heads swiveled, then hands were slowly lowered and shoulders sagged in sorrow. The silence was heavy, broken only by Zantor's shrill screams. Then came another tortured cry.

"Aa-a-gh!"

"Yanek! Bodak!" someone yelled. "Water! Hurry!"

The crowd came to life and people flew in all directions, but time was running out. Bodak and Yanek writhed in agony as flames licked at their legs.

"*Eeeiiieee!*" shrieked Zantor. "*Eeeiiieee!*" The pitch of Zantor's shrieks became so high that people in the crowd began to clasp their ears and cry out in pain. Then, as Darek watched in astonishment, Zantor's cage shattered like a crystal shell and the little dragon rose up into the air. He fluttered over and dropped down into the ring of flame that surrounded Darek's father. A moment later the dragonling rose up again, tiny wings pumping furiously. Darek's father's great, limp body was clutched tightly in his claws.

Darek's father and Bodak sat sipping hot glub from steaming mugs, their bandaged feet propped up on chairs. Zantor was curled up in exhausted sleep between them, and

Yanek reached down and stroked his small head affectionately.

The little dragon stirred. "*Thrrummm,*" he mumbled tiredly.

Bodak smiled. "You know, Yanek," he said, "I still can't quite believe I'm sitting here."

Yanek nodded and looked over at Darek. Love and pride glowed in his eyes. "Aye," he said, shaking his head in wonder, "neither can I, but I guess when you have a son who has the makings of a great leader, anything is possible."

Darek smiled back, warmed by his father's words, but a little bit frightened too. Leadership, he had discovered, could be a pretty scary business. Maybe he *would* be a leader someday, but for now he just wanted to be a boy again, a boy with a dragon in the family.

Dragon Quest

To my brother, Richard, with love

Prologue

When Darek's father and brother went off with the other hunters on a dragon quest, Darek wished with all his heart that he could have gone, too. Like all the other boys his age, Darek dreamed of being a hero and fighting a dragon. When the hunters returned with a slain Great Blue, the largest and fiercest of all dragons, the villagers gave them all a hero's welcome. Darek thought the hunters were heroes, too, until he found a baby dragon hiding in the dead Great Blue's pouch. The dragonling was so small and

frightened that Darek felt sorry for it and decided to take it back to the Valley of the Dragons. There, Darek made a startling discovery.
Dragons were peace-loving creatures and killed
only in self-defense.

Darek gave the baby dragon a powerful name,
Zantor, and brought it back to his village. But
the other Zorians did not welcome the dragonling. They nearly put Zantor to death, and
Darek's father, too! With the help of his best
friend, Pola, Darek finally managed to convince
the villagers of the truth about dragons, but it
was almost too late. The executions had begun!
At the last moment, young Zantor proved that
he was worthy of his name, saving himself and
Darek's father.

Now Darek, Pola, and Zantor are the heroes,
and all seems peaceful at last, but Darek's father
is still worried. "Such things are not always as
simple as they seem," he warns.

1

Darek pointed a stick toward the sky. He swung it in two wide circles, then slowly lowered it until its point touched the ground. Above his head, Zantor soared, following the pattern Darek had traced in the air. The dragonling circled once, then twice over the paddock. Then he swooped down for a landing.

"Hooray!" Darek shouted. He and his best friend, Pola, clapped excitedly. "That was perfect!"

The little dragon barreled across the field in

his funny, lopsided gait. Joyfully, he hurled himself at Darek, knocking him backward into the dirt. Darek squirmed with laughter as Zantor covered his face with kisses, *Thwip! Thwip!* The forked tongue tickled! Darek pulled a sugar cube from his pocket and tossed it a few feet away. The dragon scuffled after it, and Darek got to his feet and dusted himself off. Pola was still laughing, but he wasn't the only one, Darek realized. He turned and saw that he, Pola, and Zantor had an audience. A group of village children were hanging over the paddock fence.

"Zantor! Zantor, come here!" they cried, reaching out eager hands. When Zantor waddled over to play, the children shrieked with delight. "Let me pet him first!" one cried out. "No, me! No, me!" the others shouted.

Darek frowned. He was pleased, of course, that the villagers had finally accepted Zantor. For a time, it had seemed that they wouldn't even let him *live*. But Zantor had proven to all that he was both peaceful and courageous, and now they were willing to let him live among them. In fact, Zantor had become so popular lately that Darek seemed to be forever fighting for the dragonling's attention. Darek was the one who had found Zantor, after all, and brought him to the village. Why should he have to share him now with people who hadn't even wanted him at first? It didn't seem fair.

"Hey." Pola nudged Darek in the ribs. "Look who's here."

Darek looked where Pola had nodded. A taller girl had joined the other children. Her long, dark hair fell over her shoulders as she reached out and scratched the horn nubs on Zantor's head.

Zantor buried his face in the girl's shining hair and *thrummed* happily. Darek's frown deepened. "Rowena," he said with a groan.

Pola grinned. "I think she likes you," he said. "She's always hanging around lately."

"It's not me she likes, it's *him*," Darek said. "Besides, who cares?"

"She's awful pretty," Pola teased.

"Yeah," Darek agreed, "and she's awful headstrong, stuck-up, and spoiled."

Pola laughed. "Maybe you'd be headstrong, stuck-up, and spoiled, too, if *your* father was Chief Elder."

Darek snorted. Then, as he watched Zantor playing with Rowena, a strange thing began to happen. Happy little thoughts started pushing into Darek's head. They seemed to swell and pop, one after another, like bubbles. For a moment, Darek swore he could smell the perfume of Rowena's hair. He could almost feel the touch of her hands. Then, just as quickly as the funny feelings had come, they were gone. Confused, Darek shook his head.

"What's wrong?" Pola asked.

"I . . . it's weird," Darek said. "I felt like I was inside Zantor's head for a minute."

Pola looked over at Zantor and Rowena and laughed out loud. "Sounds like wishful thinking to me," he said. Then he gave Darek another poke.

Darek's frown returned. If he *had* been inside Zantor's head, he didn't like what he had felt there. Zantor was growing way too fond of Rowena. "Zantor!" he shouted. "Get back over here."

Rowena wound her arms tightly around the dragon. Zantor glanced over at Darek but didn't try to break free.

"Now!" Darek boomed.

With a sudden jerk, Zantor broke away from Rowena. He scuffled over to Darek as fast as his little legs would carry him. Darek looked at Rowena and grinned, as if to say, "See, he's all mine." Rowena glared back, tossing her head.

"I was just petting him," she called. "You don't have to be so mean about it."

"Zantor's not a pet," Darek snapped. "He and I have work to do. If you want to pet something, go pet a yuke."

Rowena glared a moment longer, then turned and stormed away.

Pola looked at Darek and shook his head.

"What's wrong with you?" Darek asked.

"You have a funny way of showing a girl that you like her," Pola said.

"I *don't* like her," Darek insisted. "She's nothing but a pest."

"Oh, yeah?" Pola said. He laughed and pointed to Zantor. The dragonling was still gazing, dreamy-eyed, after Rowena. "Doesn't look like Zantor agrees with you."

2

"You should have seen Zantor today," Darek said to his mother and father and his brother, Clep, over dinner. "He's learning so fast! He takes off and lands on command. He can fly a circle and a figure eight . . ."

Hearing his name, Zantor uncurled himself from the hearth. He shuffled over and nuzzled Darek's arm. *"Thrumm,"* he sang happily at Darek's elbow. Darek smiled and slipped him a spoonful of barliberry pudding.

Darek's mother, Alayah, attempted to frown.

"No feeding the dragon at the table," she reminded her son.

Darek's father ate quietly. He listened but did not respond to Darek's chatter. Yanek had come to accept Zantor. He even loved the little dragon, but at the same time he had doubts about Darek's dream. A future where people and dragons lived peacefully, side by side, helping each other?

"It's a nice idea," Yanek would say when Darek pressed him about it. "But such things are not always as simple as they seem."

It was true that such things *weren't* simple. Darek had learned that the hard way. When his father had allowed Darek to bring Zantor back to Zoriak, the villagers had been very angry. They had almost burned Yanek at the stake! But Darek and Zantor had proved to the villagers that they were wrong about dragons. One day, Darek was sure, he and Zantor would prove his father wrong about the future, too.

Darek turned toward his big brother. "Hurry

and finish eating, Clep," he said. "I want to show you everything Zantor learned today."

Clep was just swallowing his last spoonful of pudding when a sharp rap came on the door.

"I'll get it," Darek said, jumping up.

He pulled the door open, then stepped back in surprise. "Excellency," he said, bowing low. The Chief Elder himself stood on their doorstep.

Darek's parents and Clep quickly rose to their feet.

His mother rushed forward. "Enter, Sire," she said. "Please take some supper with us."

"I have already supped, Alayah," the Elder said. He nodded stiffly to them all. "I have come to have a word with Yanek."

"Of course." Darek's father bowed and led the way to the front parlor.

Darek and Clep glanced uneasily at each other.

Alayah twisted her apron in her hands. "I hope this visit does not bode ill," she whispered to her sons.

"As you know," they overheard the Chief Elder say, "my daughter's Decanum approaches."

Darek sighed a sigh of relief. So that was all. The Chief Elder had come to talk over the arrangements for Rowena's Decanum. The whole village was soon to celebrate her tenth birthday. There would be a full parade, a banquet, and a formal ball. Darek's father, as Chief Marksman and Captain of the Guard, would have much to do to prepare.

Darek's mother seemed relieved, too. She went back to the table to finish her pudding.

"You know, Darek," she said with a teasing smile, "there has been much talk in the village. Everyone is wondering who Rowena will choose to be her escort for the Decanum Ball."

Darek's face reddened. Rowena's escort? What was his mother getting at?

"Have *you* any idea who her escort will be?" she asked.

"Not at all," Darek answered shortly.

Clep grinned. "I've heard some names mentioned, Mother," he said. "One very familiar name, in fact." He shot a teasing glance at Darek. "Perhaps that explains the Chief Elder's visit, eh?"

Darek gave Clep such a look of dismay that Clep had to laugh out loud. "It's not the end of the world, little brother," he said. "I can think of fates worse than having to dance with the lovely Rowena."

"Why don't *you* escort her if you think she's so lovely?" Darek snapped. "I think she's a spoiled brat."

"Hush, you two!" Alayah whispered. "Have you forgotten who speaks with your father in the next room?"

Zantor bounced over and butted Darek in the arm. Glad of the interruption, Darek went to the cupboard. He took out the dragonling's bowl and began to prepare his supper.

"It makes no difference what you think, Darek," Clep said in a more serious voice. "You will, of course, accept if you are asked."

Darek didn't answer. He filled Zantor's bowl with fallow meal and barliberries. Then he ladled warm water over all and stirred it into a mash. The smell of it suddenly made his stom-

ach growl hungrily. He raised the bowl to his lips and took a big gulp.

"Blaah!" It tasted awful. Darek spit the mash back into the bowl and stared at it. What on Zoriak had possessed him to eat Zantor's food? He'd just finished eating his own dinner! And even if he was hungry, he would never eat fallow meal mash! He looked up and saw Clep and his mother staring at him strangely.

"What *are* you doing?" his mother asked.

Zantor butted Darek's arm again, nearly upsetting the bowl. Darek lowered it slowly to the floor. The dragonling dived eagerly for the food, gulping and gulping. Slowly, the hunger pangs in Darek's stomach began to subside.

"I know what he's doing, Mother," Clep said. "He's trying to change the subject."

"What subject?" Darek mumbled, still staring at Zantor. The dish was nearly empty now, and Darek was feeling quite full. A bubble swelled and swelled in his stomach. It wiggled its way up through his chest and burst from his mouth. "Bu-urp!"

"Darek!" his mother exclaimed.

Darek clapped a hand over his mouth. "Sorry," he muttered. What was happening to him?

Clep frowned and shook his head. "Why would anyone want to go to the ball with a dragon-wit like you, anyway?" he asked.

"I'm sure Rowena *doesn't* want to go with me," Darek retorted. "Why do you even listen to those stupid rumors?"

"*Ahem.*"

Darek looked up at the sound of the deep voice. His father's broad frame filled the doorway. He was staring at Darek with a serious look on his face.

"You had better come in here, son," he said. "The Chief Elder's mission today concerns you."

Darek swallowed hard and stared at his father.

"Go on with you," Clep said, grinning broadly and giving Darek a little push toward the parlor. Darek stumbled a few steps, then recovered and followed his father in silence. The Chief Elder stood waiting, tall and stern.

"I've a question to put to you, boy," he said as Darek approached.

Darek's heart sank. He lowered his eyes and nodded. "I . . . I would be honored, Sire," he mumbled.

"Honored?" the Elder repeated. "Honored to do what?"

Darek glanced up at his father and then back at the Elder.

"Why . . . to escort Rowena to the ball, Sire," he said. "Isn't that why you're here?"

The Elder's lips twitched. A glint of humor sparkled in his eyes. "You flatter yourself, son," he said. "My daughter sent me on no such mission."

Darek wanted to faint with relief. The Chief Elder's mission had nothing to do with the Decanum Ball! He wouldn't have to dance with Rowena after all. But then a warm flush of embarrassment crept up his neck. What a fool he had made of himself!

"I'm sorry, Sire," he mumbled. "What is it that you wished to discuss with me?"

The Elder folded his arms across his chest, and his long robes gathered around him. "I want your dragon," he said. "I came to buy Zantor."

146

3

Darek's eyes opened wide. Could he have heard right?

"You . . . you want to *buy* Zantor?" he stammered.

"Yes." The Chief Elder began to pace. His mood seemed suddenly to turn sour. "I never dreamed I'd allow one of the nasty creatures into my household," he said. "But Rowena has taken a fancy to the beast and will have nothing else. I wouldn't give the matter a second thought if it weren't her Decanum. One must . . . make allowances at such a time." He rolled his eyes at Darek's father. "You are a father, too, Yanek," he said. "I'm sure you can understand."

"Well I do, Sire," Yanek said, nodding.

The Elder stopped pacing and turned to Darek. "Name your price, boy," he said. "And mind you, be fair about it."

Darek's mouth dropped open. "But I *can't* sell Zantor," he said. "I mean, he's not for sale."

The Elder's brows crashed together. "Not for sale?" he boomed. "What do you mean, not for sale? Everything is for sale. Don't be trying to cheat me, boy—driving the price up. I'll have you in the stocks!"

"No, Sire," Darek blurted. "I'm not. It's just that . . . Zantor isn't a *thing,* he's my friend. I can't sell him. I . . . I don't own him. Dragons can't be *owned.*"

"Barli rot!" the Elder bellowed. "Your father said I must speak to you. Now, name your price and be quick about it!"

Darek glanced at his father and swallowed hard. Then he took a deep breath and bravely returned the Elder's stare. "I . . . I don't own him," he repeated. "He followed me home from the Valley of the Dragons of his own free will. He stays with me because he wants to. He's my friend. That's all."

The Chief Elder's eyes blazed. "Yanek," he said, turning to Darek's father, "I grow weary of your son's impertinence. Name me a price for the beast, and let me be on my way. I've more important matters to attend to."

Yanek glanced at Darek. Darek pleaded with his eyes, begging his father to understand. Inside, he could feel himself trembling. He remembered all too well what had happened the last time his father had defied the Chief Elder.

At last, Yanek drew in a deep breath and bowed to the Elder. "My apologies, Sire," he said. "But if my son says the beast is not for sale, I fear it is not for sale."

The Chief Elder's eyes widened, then narrowed down to angry slits. His nostrils flared. "Fine, then," he spat. "In that case, Yanek, you will ready your men for a dragon quest on the morrow. Be prepared to leave at dawn for the Valley of the Dragons. There you will stay until you have captured a dragonling for my daughter's Decanum." He leaned forward and pressed a finger hard into Yanek's chest. "And it had better be a Great Blue!"

With that, the Elder turned and strode from the room, his royal robes billowing out behind him.

4

Darek ran across the paddock after his father, tugging at the sleeve of his jerkin. "Please, Father," he begged. "You can't do this. It isn't right."

"Darek," his father said, "I am weary of discussing this with you. The Council of Elders decides what is right and wrong. I am Captain of the Guard. I must follow the orders of the Council."

"But you're an Elder yourself," Darek argued.

"With one vote," his father reminded him.

"But you can convince the others . . ."

Darek's father stopped and stared down at Darek. "Convince them of what? That my son should have a dragon and the Chief Elder's daughter should not?"

"But Zantor chose to be with me. No one *captured* him. It isn't the same," Darek argued.

Yanek shook his head. "I'll do my best to try and prevent bloodshed," he said quietly. "That's all I can promise."

Darek saw the expression in his father's eyes and realized that it was senseless to argue further. Yanek did not approve of this mission, either. But nothing would keep him from doing his duty. Darek sighed and nodded. "Can I go along, at least?" he asked.

"I'm sorry," Yanek said. "You're to stay here, with your mother." Then he strode over to where Clep and the others stood waiting in the early morning light.

Yanek gave the order to mount, and the dragon quest party rode out. Throngs of villagers followed them to the edge of town, cheering and wishing them well. Just like the old days, Darek thought, when the men used to hunt dragons. Darek had hoped those days were gone forever. Zantor shuffled over to him.

"*Rrrronk*," he cried.

Darek stared sadly at the little dragon. Zantor's own mother had been killed brutally, needlessly, on just such a dragon quest. "I'm sorry, my friend," Darek said quietly.

Suddenly, from across the paddock there came a soft call. "Zantor . . . Zantor, come here, fella!"

Zantor's ears pricked up, and Darek whirled around.

Rowena! How dare she come here now?

"Stay," Darek commanded in a low growl, but

it was too late. Zantor was already half running, half flying toward the girl. Darek ran after him, but by the time he reached Rowena and the dragon, they were already snuggling together.

"Zantor!" Darek shouted, stomping his foot. "Come here!"

Zantor glanced at Darek but did not pull away. Rowena twined her arms around the little dragon's neck and kissed him on the nose. Zantor looked up at her, his green eyes shining.

"Soon we'll have a new friend!" she told him excitedly. "Another little dragon to play with."

"Thrummm," Zantor sang happily.

Darek was so angry at Rowena he felt like he could breathe fire.

"A friend!" he spat. "Do you steal a *friend* from its mother, Rowena? Do you tear it from its family? Force it to leave its home? Is that how you treat your *friends,* Rowena?"

Rowena glared at him. "That's what *you* did, isn't it?" she asked innocently.

"You know full well it's not," Darek snapped. "Zantor's mother was dead when I found him. She was killed on a dragon quest. He came with me because he chose to."

Rowena tossed her head. "And my dragon will choose to be with me," she said. Then she hugged Zantor tighter and narrowed her eyes. "Just like Zantor would, if you'd *let* him. Wouldn't you, Zantor?"

Zantor stared at her with adoring eyes. *Thwip!* Out flicked his tongue, planting a kiss on her cheek.

Suddenly, all of Darek's anger melted, and he felt a rush of tenderness toward Rowena. She seemed to be the sweetest, loveliest creature he had ever seen. Before he knew it, *he* was kissing Rowena on the cheek, too!

"What are you *doing,* you dragon-wit!" she shrieked. She gave Darek a shove, and he sprawled on his back in the dirt. He lay there staring at the sky, his head spinning. Did he . . . ? Had he just . . . ? No. He couldn't

have. It must have been a dream. He turned and looked. Rowena was gone.

Yeah, that's what it was, he told himself. A terrible, horrible dream. That's all. But . . . then . . . if it *was* just a dream, why did he feel like *thrumming?*

5

Darek couldn't sleep. He was too confused. And too angry with that . . . girl! She had no idea how much trouble she was causing. She had never been to the Valley of the Dragons. She didn't know how beautiful it was, how majestic the dragons were at peace.

A dragon quest! Darek shuddered at the thought. What did Rowena know of the horrors of battle? Had she ever ached over the loss of a dear one the way Darek still ached over Yoran? Yoran had been Clep's best friend. He'd been like a third brother in their house as long as Darek could remember. But now he was dead. Killed on the last dragon quest, like so many other young men before him. Killed fighting a dragon that only wished to be left alone. Yoran had died fighting Zantor's mother. And she had died, too, defending her baby, Zantor. Now other dragons might die. And men, too, maybe even his father or Clep. All for the foolish whim of a spoiled, selfish girl.

Darek sat up and threw his covers aside. At the foot of the bed, Zantor stirred, instantly alert. Darek couldn't stand it any longer—doing nothing. Even now a battle might be raging. He had stopped a battle once. Maybe he could do so again. His father would be angry with him if he disobeyed, but Darek had to follow his heart. He had always followed his heart, and it had not yet led him astray. He dressed quickly and pushed his bedroom window open. Then he motioned for Zantor to come to him.

"Hush," he whispered, pressing a finger to his lips. He stared directly into the little dragon's eyes. How could he explain to Zantor what he wanted him to do? He touched Zantor's chest, then his own, then pointed to the ground, two stories below. "I want you to fly me down there," he said.

Zantor looked out the window and then back at Darek. Goose bumps broke out on Darek's skin as he saw a light dawn in the dragon's eyes. Zantor understood! They were communicating somehow, mind to mind. Darek had little time to ponder this wonder, for Zantor quickly sprang into action. He leaped to the window ledge and fluttered out into the night. Slowly, he began to circle, then picked up speed. Darek climbed out and crouched on the windowsill, waiting. He had no doubt that Zantor could do what he'd asked. Small as the dragon was, he was capable of enormous, if brief, bursts of power. Darek had seen him carry things many times his own weight.

Zantor circled twice more, then somehow Darek knew the time was right. Just as Zantor swooped by, Darek leaned forward, and the dragonling plucked him neatly from the ledge. Together, they fluttered toward the ground. Zantor's wings pumped mightily as his claws gently grasped Darek's arms.

"You did it!" Darek praised him when they touched down safely. "Good boy."

"*Thrummm, thrummm,*" Zantor sang, glowing with pride.

Motioning the dragonling to follow, Darek crept around to the stables. He chose two strong, young yukes and led them outside. They began to fret in the darkness, but he calmed them with sugar cubes and saddled them. He climbed up on one and grabbed the other's reins.

"C'mon, Zantor," he whispered. "Let's go get Pola."

Zantor took to the air and followed at close range.

Pola's bedroom was on the ground floor of
his family's home. A light rap on his window
quickly woke him. It took no more than a word
from Darek to persuade him to come along.
Pola never was one to resist an adventure. He
was dressed in an instant, and they were off.

The going was slow at first because of the darkness, but once the sun rose, Darek, Pola, and Zantor made better time. By midday, they had reached the Black Mountains of Krad.

"We're about halfway to the Valley of the Dragons," Darek announced. He eyed the Black Mountains warily as they skirted the smoke-shrouded crags. The trees and grasses on the mountainsides had died long ago. Nothing was visible through the haze but twisted stumps and jagged rocks. "Lord Eternal, those mountains are creepy," Darek said.

Pola nodded, shivering in the shadows of the peaks. "I get the feeling that something—or *someone*—is up there watching," he said. "Don't you?"

Darek laughed. "Kradens?" he asked.

Pola laughed, too. Zorian legends told of Kradens, fierce, hairy men who had supposedly driven the Zorians' ancestors out of Krad long ago. "You don't believe those old myths, do you?" Pola asked.

Darek snorted. "What do you take me for, a nurseling? Of course I don't believe those old wives' tales."

"It's supposed to be true that our ancestors came out of those mountains in the Beginning, though," Pola said.

Darek shrugged. "It's hard to believe anything alive could come out of there," he said.

"They weren't always black and dead," Pola reminded him. "It is said that in the Beginning, they were just as beautiful as the Yellow Mountains of Orr."

Darek stared hard at the forbidding peaks. "If that's true," he wondered aloud, "then what caused them to die?"

"I don't know," Pola said. "But I'd sure like to go up there and try to find out."

Darek whirled to look at his friend. "Are you joking?" he asked. "You know it's forbidden to go up there."

Pola laughed. "Oh, and you never do *anything* forbidden, do you?" he teased. "Might I remind you that we're on a forbidden quest right now?"

"That's different," Darek said.

"Different how?"

Darek turned serious. "People used to go into the Black Mountains in the Long Ago," he said quietly, "but no one ever came back alive. That's why it's forbidden, Pola. Have you forgotten?"

"But nobody's gone in generations," Pola argued. "Maybe things have changed."

"Yeah." Darek nodded toward the mountains. "For the worse. Only a fool would go up there, Pola."

Pola was quiet for a while. There was no sound but the *clip-clop* of yuke hooves and the rush of wings as Zantor soared overhead. An acrid smell hung in the air, though, a smell like death.

"What if . . . what if the ones who went didn't come back because it's so nice there?" Pola said at last. "What if they didn't come back because they didn't *want* to come back?"

Darek laughed out loud. "Nice?" he said. "Does anything about those mountains look *nice* to you? Besides, if it was so nice, don't you think *someone* would come back and tell the rest of us?"

Pola smiled. "Yeah, I guess you're right," he said. Then he gazed back over his shoulder. "Sure would be a great adventure, though, wouldn't it?"

6

Darek, Pola, and Zantor reached the Yellow Mountains of Orr by night. The campfires of the Zorian hunting party flickered on a ridge about halfway up the slopes. Darek and Pola made their own camp well below. To be sure they wouldn't be seen, they went without a campfire. At dawn, they skirted the main path and found another way up the peaks, leaving the yukes tied below. Darek looped a halter around Zantor's neck to keep him close.

"Easy, now, easy," he whispered. "This is just

to keep you safe, my friend." Zantor did not object. He seemed to sense the danger and put his trust in Darek. Carefully, quietly, the three climbed the last few hundred feet.

"Wow!" Pola exclaimed when they finally reached the top.

"*Thrummm,*" Zantor sang softly as he gazed once again upon the valley of his birth.

"I told you it was beautiful," Darek whispered.

"I've never seen anything so beautiful in all my life," Pola agreed in a hushed voice.

Everything was peaceful in the valley. Although they had a day's head start, the hunting party had apparently made no move as yet. Darek was not surprised. His father had promised to try to avoid bloodshed. To do so, the hunters would have to lie low and watch the dragons' movements for some time. They would have to wait for just the right moment to sneak in and do their dirty work. Only then would they stand a chance of escaping. Even so, it would not be easy.

The mountains around the valley sparkled. The soft, violet rays of the morning sun bathed them in pale hues of blue and rose. Dragons perched on the crags like great, colorful blossoms. Others soared in graceful circles through the air. Still others grazed peacefully on the valley floor. Darek saw Yellow Crested dragons, and Green Horned, and also a few small Purple Spotted. The dreaded Red Fanged and Purple Spiked that once struck terror into the hearts of all Zorians were completely gone. Zorians had hunted them to extinction. It was the Red Fanged and Purple Spiked that had long ago given dragons a bad name, Darek was certain.

"Where are the Blues?" Pola asked.

Darek searched the valley, troubled by this question. "I don't know," he said. "I saw only one female and her three dragonlings when last I came. She lived in that cave high up on the mountainside there." Darek pointed. "I'd hoped there were others, off hunting or something, but I see no Blues again today."

"The Great Blues have been the favored game of the dragon quests ever since the Red Fanged and Purple Spiked disappeared," Pola said. "Can it be that they are nearly extinct now, too?"

Darek looked at Zantor and swallowed hard. He had not thought of this before. "I pray not," he said quietly.

Pola gazed thoughtfully out over the valley. "Two males were taken in the dragon quest before last," he said. "They could have been the fathers of Zantor and the other three."

Darek felt a sinking in his heart as he recognized the likely truth of Pola's words. "Yes," he said quietly. "They could, indeed."

"The other three young ones . . ." Pola said. "Are they males or females?"

Darek thought back to his earlier trip to the valley. He had spent time in the Great Blue's cave, trying to get her to adopt Zantor. He remembered that the Great Blue's dragonlings had pouches like their mother. "They are females all," he said.

Zantor suddenly sprang upright and started thrumming wildly. Darek tightened his halter and pulled him close.

"Rrronk! Rrronk!" he cried, struggling to get free.

"Shush, shush, Zantor, no!" Darek cried in his ear. "You have to stay still."

The dragonling quieted, but Darek sensed his longing as he stared out across the valley.

"Look!" Pola whispered.

So that was what Zantor was so excited about. The Great Blue was emerging from her cave! She unfurled her silvery wings and stretched them out full-length. She stepped to the edge of the cliff and sprang off as lightly as a bird. Out against the sky she soared, blue on blue. The sun glinted and danced on her wings as she circled nearly over their heads.

"She's magnificent," Pola said.

"*Thrummm,*" Zantor sang, looking up.

"Yes." Darek smiled and rubbed the little dragon's head. "One day, you will be just as magnificent, my friend."

One by one, the three smaller Blues appeared at the cave mouth and fluttered out after their mother. Darek smiled, happy to see that they were all still there and healthy. Then, like a cloud across the sun, a new thought came to him.

"Pola," he whispered, "if what you say is true, then Zantor is the last male Blue alive."

Pola nodded somberly. "And if he doesn't grow up and mate with one of those three," he added, "they will be the last Blues . . . *ever*."

As if he clearly understood Darek and Pola's words, Zantor looked up at them with mournful eyes. "*Rrronk,*" he cried softly.

7

Nothing moved on the ridge through all the long, hot day. Pola went back to the yukes to get the water skins, then took Zantor with him in search of food and fresh water. He returned with an assortment of nuts and berries and the two bulging skins. Darek drank deeply and squirted a little of the refreshing liquid over his sun-scorched head. Zantor curled up to sleep in the shade of an outcropping of rock. As the afternoon dragged on, Darek and Pola dozed, too.

"Do you think the hunting party will try anything today?" Pola asked when they woke.

Darek stretched and looked at the sky. "I don't know," he said. "If they do, it should be soon. The dragons will be waking from their afternoon naps shortly."

"Why is that a good time?" Pola asked.

"The adults wake first," Darek explained. "They go off to forage for dinner while their little ones are still asleep."

"But how will our men capture a dragonling without causing a ruckus?" Pola asked.

Darek shook his head. That he didn't know. He feared to think what might happen if things went wrong. Dragons were peaceful if left alone, but they were fierce and dangerous when threatened. Their fiery breath and razor-sharp claws had sent many a Zorian to an early death. Darek prayed to Lord Eternal that his father had a plan.

True to Darek's words, the adult dragons soon began emerging from their caves and drifting down into the valley. Before long, the Great Blue appeared. She flew to the valley's far end and disappeared into the thick forest. Sadly, Darek watched her go. She had no idea of the danger threatening her young ones.

Darek still clearly remembered his first meeting with her. She had been ready to defend her babies with her very life. She was a mother, after all, as loving as any human mother. He didn't like to think of the pain and loss she must suffer now because of Rowena. New anger at the girl flared inside him as he watched the mouth of the cave. The little ones were in there, probably still sleeping, just as Zantor still snored beneath his rock. If the hunting party planned to act today, now would be the time.

"Look!" Pola whispered. He pointed to the ridge above the cave.

For a moment, Darek couldn't believe what he saw there. Another Great Blue had appeared! It was a male, small for a Blue, but definitely full-grown. The shape of the head and the color of the scales were unmistakable. As Darek and Pola watched, the new dragon started to move down the mountain face. But something was wrong. It didn't have an adult dragon's strong, high-stepping gait. Instead, it moved in a sluggish, awkward fashion, almost as if it were dragging itself.

"Lord Eternal!" Darek whispered. "It's a decoy!"

He and Pola stared at each other in astonishment. "They must have made it from one of the dragon-skin hangings in Elder Hall," Pola said.

Darek smiled and shook his head in wonderment. What a wise man his father was!

"Do you think it could possibly work?" Pola asked.

Darek felt torn as he watched the awkward creature lurch into the mouth of the cave. He'd been against the whole quest from the start, and his heart wanted it to fail. But his head knew that lives were on the line, including his father's and Clep's. If this plan didn't work, there would

surely be bloodshed and death before the day was over. He grabbed Pola's arm and squeezed tight. "Pray," he whispered.

Not one, but all three little dragons followed the strange new Blue out of their cave and up over the ridge. Darek and Pola moved around the mountain, closer to the hunting party's encampment, to get a better look. Zantor had awakened, and Darek was having trouble controlling him.

"Easy, fella, easy," Darek whispered. "I know you want to go to them, but you can't just now."

"*Rrronk,*" the dragonling replied.

The odd procession was coming closer and closer, making its way down the back side of the mountain. Strange emotions tumbled through Darek's mind as Zantor *thrummed* and tugged on his halter.

"Easy," Darek repeated, but he now felt drawn to the procession, too. The need to be with the other dragons was becoming an ache inside him. He found himself itching to let Zantor go.

"Here," he said, handing the halter to Pola. "You'd better hold him. I'm not sure I can trust myself."

Pola looked at him strangely. "Trust yourself to do what?"

"I feel like I'm inside Zantor's head again," Darek said.

Pola arched an eyebrow. "What are you talking about?"

Darek shook his head. "I'll explain later," he said. "Just hold him—tight."

Pola took the tether and wrapped it tightly around his wrist. Zantor's head sagged, and Darek felt the dragonling's disappointment as keenly as if it were his own. He turned away and tried to concentrate on the procession.

"Do you think they're going to take all three?" Pola asked.

"I'm afraid they'll have to now," Darek said. "If they try to separate them, there'll be a ruckus for sure. And that would bring the mother in no time."

"Won't she follow anyway?" Pola asked.

"Not for a while," Darek said. "The dragonlings are old enough to forage for themselves. She probably won't miss them until nightfall when they don't return to the cave." A picture of the distressed mother dragon flashed into Darek's mind. She would be so worried about her young ones. If only there were some way to stop this cruel quest.

"But nightfall is only four or five hours away," Pola said.

Darek shrugged. "That's all the head start the hunting party can hope for," he said. "That, and the chance that it will take her a while to pick up the trail. It's all rock up on the mountain, so there won't be footprints, and dragons don't have much sense of smell."

"Maybe she *won't* pick up the trail," Pola said hopefully. "Maybe she'll think they're lost in the valley somewhere."

"Maybe," Darek said, but he was doubtful.

Suddenly, Zantor gave a quick twist, yanking the halter free. With a sharp cry of glee, he took to the air and zoomed straight toward the dragon procession.

"Hooray!" Darek shouted, leaping joyfully into the air. Then he crouched down and clapped his hand over his mouth.

Pola stared at him. "Have you taken leave of your senses?" he asked. "What are you yelling about? The hunting party heard you for sure!"

"I know, I know," Darek said. "I'm sorry. That wasn't me shouting, it was . . . Zantor, sort of."

Pola narrowed his eyes. "Did you get sunstroke up there today?" he asked.

Darek shook his head. "No. At least, I don't think so. Something else is going on. Something is happening in my mind. I don't understand, either, but we don't have time to worry about it right now."

Pola sighed and stared at the fleeing dragon.

"That's for sure," he said. "As soon as your father sees Zantor, he'll know for sure that we're here. What are we going to do?"

Darek thought about facing his father and the others and swallowed nervously. "You can go home," he said to Pola. "They won't know you were with me. This was all my idea, anyway. I'll . . . take the blame."

Pola stared at him a long time, then walked over to his yuke and climbed into the saddle.

"See you back home," Darek said quietly.

"No, you won't," Pola said. He leaned forward and handed the reins of the other yuke to Darek. Then he smiled. "An adventure's an adventure, all the way to the end," he said. "I'm with you, my friend."

Darek smiled and hoisted himself up into the saddle. He reached out to Pola and they clasped arms in a Brotherhood shake.

8

Darek's father's eyes were stern. "I don't care what your reason is!" he boomed. "You disobeyed an order, and you will pay the price when we return home."

"Yes, sir." Darek bowed humbly. "I'm sorry, sir."

"Aargh!" Darek's father stomped off. "Get out of my way. I've more important things to worry about."

Darek went back and stood beside Pola. They were silent for a while, watching the dragon procession. Darek felt awful, standing there, doing nothing, as the dragonlings walked into a trap. Then an idea began to take shape in his mind. If he could get close to the dragonlings, he might be able to free them. They would fly straight back to their mother. Maybe then the men would give up this foolish quest rather than risk a direct confrontation. It was a long shot. But if Darek didn't do something soon, it would be too late. He approached his father once more.

"Father," he said hesitantly. "I . . . think maybe I can help."

"Out of my sight, I told you!" his father bellowed.

Darek took a step back, but then Clep came up and put a hand on Darek's shoulder. "Wait a moment," Clep said. Then he turned to Yanek.

"A word with you, Father?" Clep asked.

Yanek stared at his two sons a long moment. Then he and Clep stepped to one side and put their heads together. Their voices rose and fell. Darek strained to catch snatches of their conversation.

"Way with dragons . . ." he heard Clep say.

"Disobedient whelp . . ." his father replied.

"Understands them . . ." Clep said.

"Taught a lesson . . ." his father grumbled.

As Darek watched his father and brother argue, his own feelings warred within him. Clep was standing up for him, taking his side. How could he let his brother down and free the dragons now? And what would the Elders do to his father if Darek made trouble again?

"Out of time . . ." he heard Clep say at last. Both Clep and Yanek turned then and looked toward the mountain. The party of dragons, now including Zantor, would soon have to be dealt with.

Yanek swore under his breath and looked over at Darek. "Do you think you can get close to those beasts without spooking them?" he asked.

"Yes, Father."

"Can you get tethers on them?"

Of this Darek wasn't so sure, but one thing he did know. "If anyone can, Father," he said, "I can."

"Well enough, then," Yanek said. "I'll settle my score with you later. Take the tethers and go."

"Yes, sir." Darek looked over at Pola, and Pola smiled back. He raised his arm and clenched his hand into a fist, palm forward. It was a Brotherhood fist. *Lord Eternal go with you*, it meant. Pola understood. He knew Darek had a difficult choice to make, and he was offering his support, no matter what Darek decided. Darek nodded his thanks to his friend. Then he started for the dragons. But what should he do? Free them or capture them?

"Son."

Darek stopped and turned. His father and Clep stood side by side. Both raised their fists as well. They trusted him, Darek realized. He felt a warm pride inside. Then, one by one, the other hunters in the party raised their Brotherhood fists, too. Darek swallowed hard. He couldn't let them down. Not now. Besides, what if he freed the dragons and the men did decide to go after them again? The capture might not go so smoothly next time.

He wasn't being a traitor to Zantor and the dragons, Darek told himself as he started up the mountain. He was just doing his best to see that no one, dragon or Zorian, got hurt.

9

Darek didn't know why the little dragons seemed so glad to see him. Did they remember him from his earlier visit to their cave, or did they take their cue from Zantor, who greeted him with nuzzles and *thrummms?* Either way, they welcomed him eagerly into their rollicking reunion with Zantor.

When Darek offered them sugar cubes, they gobbled them up and followed after him, begging for more. They were suspicious of the tethers at first, but Darek had a plan. He slipped a

tether on and off Zantor, giving him a sugar cube reward each time. Before long, the other three dragons were wearing tethers and munching on sugar cubes, too.

Soon all four dragons slept in a contented little heap in the back of a wagon pulled by Darek and Pola on their yukes. Night had fallen, and they guided the yukes carefully along a path lit only by Zoriak's twin moons. Behind them, in two columns, rode the rest of the hunting party.

Darek was glad things were going so well, but he still couldn't help worrying. It was all too easy. Much too easy. He kept watching over his shoulder for the Great Blue.

"Maybe she doesn't care," Pola said hopefully. "Maybe the dragonlings are old enough to be on their own now. Maybe she's ready to let them go."

"Maybe," Darek said. This didn't seem likely, but he *was* surprised that they had made it all the way back to the Black Mountains without any sign of the angry mother. Maybe Pola was right. Maybe he was worrying for nothing. He settled back in the saddle and allowed himself a small sigh of relief.

And then he heard it.

The shriek, though far off, sent chills up his spine. "She's coming," he whispered.

The hunting party had heard it, too.

"Circle up!" Darek heard his father shout.

The two columns behind Darek and Pola split and arched out around them. Soon the boys and the dragonlings were enclosed in a great circle.

"Now what?" Pola asked.

"Battle," Darek said bitterly. "Didn't you know it would come to this?"

The Great Blue shrieked again, closer this time. With cries of alarm, the dragonlings awoke. Darek could feel Zantor's fear. He hastily tossed some sugar cubes back into the wagon, trying to keep them all calm.

"GRRRAWWWK! GRRRAWWWK!"

The ground around them shook as the Great Blue thundered out of the sky, swooping down almost on top of her young ones.

"Rrronk! Rrronk!" the dragonlings cried, straining at their tethers.

Darek's and Pola's yukes danced and bucked.

"Control your mounts!" Darek's father shouted. "Prepare for battle. Shields up, bows ready!"

194

"GRRRAWWWK!" The Great Blue swooped again, this time letting loose a blast of flame. The little ones shrieked, and Darek's yuke reared up on its hind legs. Pola's yuke spooked and reared, too. Then, at the same time, both yukes bolted. The wagon lurched after them, bouncing over the rough ground.

"Eeeiiieee! Eeeiiieee!" the little dragonlings screamed. Their cries seemed to whip the yukes into a frenzy. Darek and Pola fought for control of the reins, but there was no holding the frightened animals back. Their hooves thundered, tearing up the ground and bathing them all in a cloud of dust.

"Get out of the way!" Darek shouted as the wagon bore down on the battle circle. Men and yukes scattered as the wagon broke through. Behind them, Darek and Pola could hear the great dragon scream as she charged once more. Sounds of a battle raged as the wagon continued to barrel out of control. It was headed straight for the Black Mountains of Krad! Fear roared in Darek's ears. His own terror, and Zantor's, too, blocked out all thought.

The wagon jounced over the foothills as the runaway yukes started up the mountain pass. Clouds of black smoke loomed ahead. The acrid smell stung Darek's nose. There was no escape. They were headed straight into the Mountains of No Return!

"Jump!" Darek shrieked to Pola as the first ghostly wisps of smoke began to drift past them. "Jump!"

At the last moment, Darek threw his reins aside and jumped. He landed with a thud and rolled over and over, coming to rest at last against a rock. He looked up just in time to see the runaway wagon and the four little dragons disappearing into the black, smoky haze.

And then he saw something else. A figure still sat astride one of the yukes!

"Pola!" Darek shrieked. *"Pola, jump!"*

But Pola didn't jump. Instead, he raised his arm high, his hand clenched in a Brotherhood fist.

"An adventure's an adventure!" he shouted.

And then they were gone . . . Pola, Zantor, all of them. Vanished.

Darek got to his feet and ran a short way into the mist. "Pola! Zantor!" he cried. But there was no answer. No sound. Darek's eyes watered, and his nose stung. He turned and staggered out of the mist again. Tears streamed down his cheeks. He turned once more and stared in stunned disbelief at the spot where the wagon had disappeared. Minutes passed. Maybe even hours. Darek didn't know. He felt empty inside, drained, as if nothing was left of his heart but an aching hole.

Then, just as dawn broke, there was a horrible, agonized cry, and the battle sounds in the distance ceased. Darek turned slowly, and the ache inside him deepened. There, on the ground, surrounded by the hunters, lay the Great Blue. The soft rays of the morning sun peeked over the mountains and glinted off her bent and lifeless wings.

10

Darek rubbed his hand across the top of Pola's Memory Stone. In time, maybe, he would be able to come here to the Memory Place and think warm thoughts, the way he did when he and Clep visited Yoran's Memory Stone. But now, all he felt was pain.

If only Zantor were still here to comfort him, to make him smile with his silly dragon antics. But Zantor was gone, too. Gone forever, along with Pola and the other three dragonlings. The Zorians would never know another Great Blue.

Darek sighed deeply. Sadness seemed to fill every corner of his mind and body, leaving no room for anything else. He slowly rose to his feet and started toward home.

"Darek?"

The voice startled him and caught him unaware. He turned, and when he saw who had spoken, his sorrow turned to something darker. Darek had never hated before, but he hated now.

"I . . . I've been waiting for a chance to speak with you," Rowena said.

Darek stared straight ahead, not trusting himself to speak.

"I . . . I want to tell you that I'm sorry," she went on. "That I . . ."

"Sorry!" Darek whirled now and faced her. "You're *sorry?*" He spat the words like fire. "You're *sorry* that my two best friends in the world are dead?"

"They're not . . . dead," Rowena said, her eyes glassy with tears. "They're just . . . gone."

Darek glared at her. "How do you know they're not dead?" he asked. "Besides, what difference does it make? I'll never see Pola or Zantor again. Pola's parents will never see their son again." He turned and gazed off into the sky, off toward the Yellow Mountains of Orr. "And no Zorian from this day forward will ever again see the beauty of a Great Blue," he added softly.

"I know . . ." Rowena's voice was almost a sob. "I'm sorry," she repeated. "What more can I say?"

Darek spun around angrily. "You're *sorry,* all right," he said in a low snarl. "You're just about the sorriest excuse for a Zorian I've ever laid eyes on." Then he turned and strode away.

11

Darek tossed and turned. Another sleepless night. He sat up and stared off toward the Black Mountains of Krad. Where were Pola and Zantor? he wondered. How were they? Were they dead or alive? Outside, he heard the clatter of yuke hooves and wondered who might be passing by at this late hour. Then something flew in through the open window and landed at the foot of his bed. The yuke hooves clattered away as Darek reached down.

It was a note, tied around a rock. Darek yanked off the twine and unfolded it.

"They are gone, not dead," it said. "I know this. Don't ask me to explain how. But I do know. And where there is life, there is hope. I ride tonight for the Black Mountains, there to undo the wrong I've done."

Darek stared at the note for a long moment until its meaning finally sank in. Rowena was heading out on a quest to find Pola and the dragons.

"Zatz!" he cried. "That fool girl!"

He pulled on his boots and his jerkin, then dashed through the sleeping house and out to the barn. He saddled the fastest yuke in the herd and flung himself onto its back. Out into the night he rode, faster and harder than he'd ever ridden before. Wind filled his mouth and tore at his hair. The yuke's hooves flew over the moon-silvered ground, tearing up league after league. At last, the Black Mountains loomed closer. Overhead, the sky grew pale with the approach of dawn.

As he bore down on the mountains, Darek spied a figure up ahead. Her loosened hair streamed wildly out behind her. Rowena and her yuke moved as one, smoothly gliding over the landscape. Darek frowned. She sat a good yuke, he had to grant her that. He spurred his yuke harder in an effort to close the gap between them, but his yuke was winded. Overtaking the girl before she reached the pass would not be easy.

"Rowena!" he screamed. *"Rowena, stop!"* But his words only blew back into his own mouth.

Rowena did not stop or even slow when she reached the foothills. On she raced toward the mist-shrouded peaks.

The acrid, dead smell of the mountains made Darek's breath catch in his throat. He was running out of time. He reached back and pulled his yuke's tether rope from behind his saddle. He played out the noose until it was the right size. Then he stood in the stirrups, swung the rope overhead a few times, and let it fly.

"Uumph!" Rowena landed on the ground with a thud. Her frightened yuke clattered off into the foothills.

"You dragon-wit!" she screamed as Darek approached. "What do you think you're doing?"

"Saving your foolish hide," Darek yelled. "Have you taken leave of your senses?"

"What is it to you?" Rowena cried. She got to her feet and slapped angrily at her dust-caked clothes.

"Are you hurt?" Darek asked.

"No, I am not hurt—no thanks to you!" Rowena turned and stomped away.

"Where are you going?" Darek shouted.

"I told you where I'm going."

"Oh, no, you're not!"

"Oh, yes, I am!"

Darek slid down off his yuke, ran up behind Rowena, and grabbed her arm. "No, you're not," he repeated. "You've caused enough trouble already . . ."

"Me!" Rowena whirled around. "And I suppose you're Sir Innocent, huh? At least *I* have the guts to admit when *I'm* wrong."

Darek stared at her. "What are you talking about?" he asked. "What did I do?"

"What *didn't* you do is more the question!" Rowena said. She pulled free and started up the mountain again. Darek ran after her once more.

"I'm listening, okay?" he said. "How is any of this my fault?"

Rowena glared at him. "If you must know the truth," she said, "I never even wanted a dragon of my own. All I wanted was a chance to spend a little time with Zantor, to play with him now and then. But you were too selfish to allow that. You were too jealous, because you knew he liked me as much as you!"

Darek's mouth dropped open. He tried to think of some sharp words to fling back at her, but he could not.

Rowena stopped walking and faced him squarely. "Did you really think you could keep

Zantor all to yourself?" she asked. "You proved to us all how wonderful he was, then you shut us out. Did you really think that was fair?"

Darek tore his eyes from Rowena's and looked down at the ground. Her words stung like the blade of a finely honed knife. And their aim was just as deadly true. He *had* been selfish and jealous. If he'd been willing to share . . .

Darek's shoulders sagged, and his arms fell limply at his sides as the truth became painfully clear. If he had been a little more considerate, Zantor and Pola might still be there.

"You're right," he said softly. "It *is* my fault. Pola . . . Zantor . . . everything."

There was a long silence, and then Rowena put a hand on his shoulder. "No," she said. "I can't let you take all the blame. I was jealous of you, too. And I behaved like a spoiled child. We are both to blame."

Darek looked up, surprised. This was a new side of Rowena, a side he had to respect. "It took guts for you to admit that," he said.

Rowena smiled and added quietly, "You've got guts, too."

"Maybe we've been wrong about each other, huh?" Darek said.

Rowena nodded. "Maybe."

It wasn't customary to offer a Brotherhood shake to a girl, but somehow it felt like the right thing to do. Darek reached out his arm. "What do you say we start over?" he asked. "Friends?"

"Friends," Rowena said. She clasped his arm and gave it a hearty shake. They smiled into each other's eyes for a moment. Then Rowena looked away. "Well," she said, "I'd better get going."

"Going where?" Darek asked.

"There." Rowena pointed into the mist.

"What?" Darek couldn't believe his ears. "You're not still going!"

"I am."

"But . . . it's forbidden," Darek said.

Rowena smiled again. "That's never stopped *you* from doing what you want," she said.

Darek shook his head. Why did everybody keep throwing that back at him?

"The things I did were important . . ." he started to say.

Rowena raised her eyebrows. "And rescuing Pola and Zantor isn't?"

Darek sighed. "Rowena," he said, "we don't even know if they're alive."

"They *are* alive," Rowena insisted. "I know."

Darek stared at her for a long moment. "Why do you keep saying that?" he asked. *"How* do you know?"

A blush of crimson stained Rowena's cheeks. "Because," she said, lowering her eyes, "Zantor . . . told me."

"Wh . . . what?" Darek stammered. A chill crept up his back.

"He . . . speaks to me," Rowena went on, "in my mind."

The chill spread out to Darek's fingers and toes. He sat down on the ground with a thud.

"I know you don't believe me—" Rowena began.

"No," Darek interrupted. He looked up at her and nodded slowly. "I do."

"You do?"

"Yes." Darek licked his lips. "He speaks to me, too."

Rowena's eyes widened. "He does? Really?"

"Yes." Darek nodded again.

"Then you've heard it!" Rowena exclaimed.

"Heard it? Heard what?"

Rowena dropped to her knees beside Darek and stared into his eyes. "Listen!"

For the first time in days, Darek pushed the heavy weight of sadness aside and opened his heart and mind. He listened, quietly, to the thoughts in his head. And then, quite clearly, he heard it! It came faintly at first, then stronger.

"*Rrronk! Rrronk! RRRONK!*"

"It *is* him," Darek whispered.

Rowena nodded.

Images started crowding into Darek's head. Dragons. Lots of dragons. The other Blues were there, and Pola, too!

"They're all together!" he shouted. "They're alive!"

Rowena smiled and nodded again.

"But where?" Darek asked. "Where?"

"Up there, somewhere," Rowena said, pointing into the mist again. Then she turned back to Darek. "And I intend to find them. Are you with me?"

Darek sat a moment longer, letting it all sink in. Then he got to his feet and stared once more at the bleak, mist-shrouded crags. Pola's last words rang in his memory: *"An adventure's an adventure!"*

"All the way to the end," Darek added softly. Then he turned to Rowena and smiled.

"Yes," he said. "I'm with you, my friend."

About the Author

Jackie French Koller is the author of over two dozen award-winning books for children and young adults, including *Nickommoh!* (Atheneum), *The Promise* (Knopf), *One Monkey Too Many* (Harcourt), and *Mole and Shrew* (Random House). The mother of three grown children, Ms. Koller wrote the first *Dragonling* book for her youngest son, Devin, because dragons were his "favorite animals, next to dogs." Jackie French Koller lives on a mountaintop in western Massachusetts with her husband and two Labrador retrievers. Visit her and Zantor on-line at http://jackiefrenchkoller.com.

BRUCE COVILLE

Author of the SPACE BRAT series

WHO THROWS THE WORLD'S GREATEST TANTRUMS?

SPACE BRAT

SPACE BRAT 2:
BLORK'S EVIL TWIN

SPACE BRAT 3:
THE WRATH OF SQUAT

SPACE BRAT 4:
PLANET OF THE DIPS

SPACE BRAT 5:
THE SABER-TOOTHED POODNOOBIE

EASY TO READ—FUN TO SOLVE!

**Meet up with suspense and mystery
in The Hardy Boys® are:**

THE CLUES™
BROTHERS

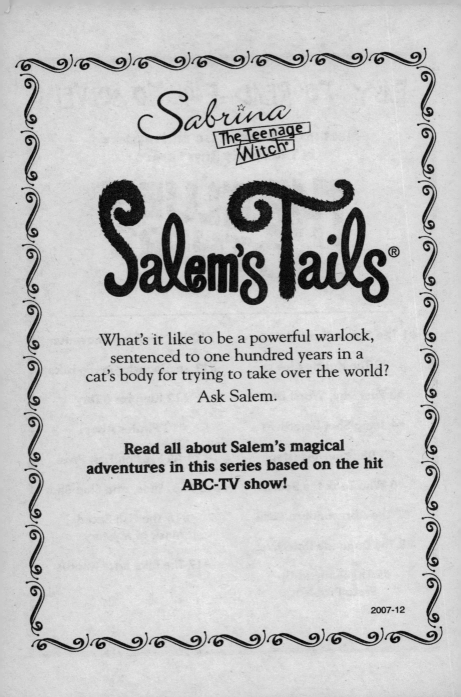